OLGA!

*What Really Happened To The
Last Tsar's Eldest Daughter*

Elizabeth Mills

Pen Press Publishers Ltd

Published in Great Britain by
Pen Press Publishers Ltd
39 Chesham Road
Brighton
E. Sussex BN2 1NB

ISBN 1-905203-88-8

Cover design Jacqueline Abromeit

Author photo © Photo Corporation (UK) Ltd

About the Author

Elizabeth Mills is a retired engineer, accounts clerk and care worker, and lives in South Yorkshire.

Contents

Rudge

Thirteen thousand years ago, in the days when the great culture of Atlantis ruled half the world, there was unrest, with wars increasing in frequency and violence. Nikolay was a strong king, a decisive leader in peace and war, and ruled well in one of the three main islands of the extensive civilisation. Ruling a neighbouring island was a clever man, tall and strong, but prone to gloom and suspicion; this man's name in modern English would be Verion Rudge. Rudge knew that Nikolay was a better king, because he used to visit Nikolay's realm in disguise, and saw the people living in peace and prosperity, while his own people, driven to distraction by his interference and meanness, spent half their time and energy thinking up plots to rid themselves of his rule. Rudge always suspected everybody else of being as unpleasant as he himself was, and could not believe that Nikolay only wanted to live in peace and harmony, so he treacherously led his army in an invasion of Nikolay's realm without any warning, but was defeated and killed by Nikolay's soldiers, who, as free men, rallied and fought better than Rudge's army of conscripts and mercenaries ever would.

Rudge went over to the other side, the spirit world where the "dead" live, and, like everybody, had a chance to think about the life he had just had and to learn what he could from it. But there is no compulsion to learn; a person can die, and go to the spirit world, and learn very little, and this is what Rudge did. Rather than admit his mistakes and move on, Rudge allowed his anger against Nikolay to grow and fester, and he ended up blaming Nikolay for all his problems, criticising him for being too good, and seeing Nikolay's goodness as naivety. He decided he was going to make Nikolay suffer in some future incarnation, so he embarked on a search through the extensive libraries and study facilities available to him in the spirit realms. After a few months he found there were methods of making sure that he would meet Nikolay in some future life, remember the fraught details of their recent clash, and become able to attack Nikolay in some way. He attached himself to a skilled teacher of mental sciences, who taught him many secrets of mind science, including a method called the Ritual of Consolidation into Memory, an old and exact method of ensuring that he would remember Nikolay and get revenge.

For the seven days of the Ritual, Rudge sat and stared at himself in a mirror, while listening to a recording of his vow of vengeance against Nikolay. Behind the words he played music chosen especially for its proven facility of creating a cell in his memory and driving it deep into his far memory, the part of the mind that every person carries with them through life after life. The memory cell would be activated in some future incarnation, either when Rudge did advanced mind training, or when he met Nikolay again, which he was bound to do sooner or later in response to his firm and unshakeable will. Desire for revenge would be reawakened, and Rudge would plan and accomplish his destruction of Nikolay according to the circumstances in which he found himself during that particular life.

King Nikolay had won the war against Rudge, but he was already seventy years old, and the Rudge War took what energy he had left. He knew that he should retire as king, for the good of his realm, and arrange the legally required election for his successor, but he could not force himself to take enough time away from his everyday duties to think things through and get round to standing down. He was tired, and suddenly he began to deteriorate mentally, spending too much time staring at jobs instead of doing them. His assistants tried to help him, but he ignored their polite advice to take some time off, and tried to hang on in his job instead of giving up. Realising that he could not do his job any more, but now unable to give it up, he began to take refuge in religion, and decided that the way to be spiritual was to stop fighting and do nothing but think of Almighty God. He could not see how wrong the decision was, nor how in thirteen thousand years' time it would cause two wars, a bloody revolution, and the deaths of a hundred million people.

In the year 1400 Common Era (also called A.D., that is Anno Domini, or Year of The Lord), a woman in southern central Asia gave birth to a son, and she and her family rejoiced, giving thanks to God for a new man to start their next generation. In modern English, the boy's name would be Verion Rudge, and he grew up, apparently normal, until he was fourteen, when he was sought and found by his magical master.

In 1414 C.E., Rudge knew very little about magic, because all that he had heard about it so far was the traditional stories of heroes and heroines, with some horror mixed in, told to him by his mother. One day while he was working at the family vegetable stall in the nearby market, his uncle, who ran the stall, gave him half an hour off to find a coffee and bread, so Rudge wandered away, and as he pottered along, a friend asked him to guard his jewellery stall for five minutes. Rudge agreed and took his place, humming a tune and hoping trade would improve so that he could impress the other lad by making one or two good sales, and maybe earn an appreciative tip.

It was then that his master came. A tall, thin man, in off-white cotton robes, bare sandalled feet, and head veiled against being seen rather than against the dust, strode to the stall, picked up a piece of jewellery, and began to talk. First he talked about the jewellery, but then he talked about Rudge, who was flattered and began to talk about his ambition to do more with his life than assist at the family

3

vegetable stall in the village for a pittance. Rudge found that he was able to be open about his desire for power, money and travel, and about his secret contempt for everybody around him.

"Human vegetables on two legs, who just accept everything and don't try to make their lives better, but I despise them. There has got to be more than this in life for me, and I intend to find it."

He stared the older man in the face, wondering why he was suddenly able to talk like this to a stranger, and noting that his friend was much slower in coming back than he had said he would be. The tall, thin, mysterious man was looking at him. Rudge stared back, and was pleased and excited, although he did not fully know why, when the man smiled for half a second, a deep, knowing look that made Rudge tingle all through with knowledge of the sudden hint of influence, wealth and power. Rudge was being weighed in a vast and merciless balance, but he did not care, rather he welcomed it, because he knew he was going to pass the test that this man was putting him through even as they both stood there by that common market stall full of cheap tat.

"There are ways to get what you want, young man, but they are only won by years of hard work, obedience and discipline."

"Sir, I want to find a way of life that does take qualities like that. I can't bear the thought of having a soft, mediocre life, manning a damned village stall until I die, never seeing what is beyond these mountains and their passes. I want a better life, travel, beautiful women, culture, and adventure, but most of all I want to stretch myself and find challenges which I think are worthy of me. Sir, do you know where I can find these things? Please tell me if you do, because I am not afraid of hardship or work."

"I may do, young man. Three evenings from now, come to my home, which is the small old house located four miles up the pass to the north-east and beyond the large carved rock this side of the bridge over the river gorge. We will take coffee and talk, and find out more about each other."

At the time, Rudge did not know that his new acquaintance was one of the leading magicians in the whole Asia-Europe landmass, but he soon began to realise how lucky he was to have been selected for his attentions and for the chance to learn from him. The man drilled Rudge and eight other young men, and two women, without mercy. Three evenings a week, after their day's work was done, the students found their way, sometimes in the teeth of huge and ignorant family hostility, to the secret rendezvous, a hidden cave entered behind a waterfall near the man's home, where they embarked on their studies, which they referred to as their real life, their life in magic.

"If you want something, and really want it, and have decided that you have to have it, do not let anything or anybody stop you. Human lives, animal lives, what are they to you? Sacrifice them if you have to, and pour out the blood on to the ground, and make offering to the old gods, the steadfast ones who will give you what you want when you make the blood sacrifice, and no nonsense about having to live in poverty or having scruples about how you get what you want. No. Mark this, my young and valued friends: the old gods admire people like you, because you have decided to tell the universe what you want and make it give it all to you."

The first time that Rudge was invited, which he knew meant ordered, to kill the sacrificial bird and pour its blood out over the heads of his fellow students, he had to swallow hard, but he forced himself to do the act because everybody else was watching and he dare not swallow for a second time because the master would notice and probably throw him permanently out of the study group. Gradually, any knowledge which he might have had about good versus evil faded from his mind, and under the encouragement of the master he decided that what he himself wanted was

5

automatically good and should be pursued regardless, whether he wanted material things like wealth, or mental things like influence. Thus he passed, first unconsciously and then deliberately, across the great divide into what has always been called the Practice of the Left Hand Path.

By the age of thirty, Verion Rudge had learnt all that he could from his first teacher. With a glowing letter of recommendation, which he knew was backed up by telepathic messages, he travelled to one of the world's foremost centres of magical study to carry on developing himself and pursuing his ambitions, which were by now crystallising into a desire for political power. Low grade aspirations such as ownership of things or people interested him not one iota. What he wanted was to hold the lives of masses of people in his hand and manipulate, change, or use them for his own ends, which, he was now beginning to realise, were to plunge people into and out of suffering and joy, poverty and wealth, and sickness and health at a whim for his own amusement, studying the people rather as a normal person would watch a rat in a trap, because to Rudge by now, people were of no more value than rats. He studied and practised, learning and confirming what he had already suspected, namely that war, peace, famine and plenty did not just happen, but were controlled by a small group of people who stayed hidden behind a range of fronts worldwide. He learned that it was possible, by high magical practice, to prolong his life to many times what was considered possible to ordinary people, and he decided he was going to become one of that group of hidden manipulators.

The Centre of Magical Sciences was founded half a million years ago as a colony of Lemuria, that strange lost continent long since sunk below the Pacific Ocean. Old, the Centre was, but vibrant and ever new. Stunningly high buildings reared above the traveller. Located near a major road through high mountains, the Centre brooded, its sinister rays contaminating the land. It was filled with the most expert of the world's evil magicians. Within its walls grew the conspiracies of the centuries. Those who studied there were the elite of the elite, and those who ruled there were merciless.

Brother Rudge fitted in well. Soon his tall, gaunt figure was seen at the most important lectures and workshops. He knew that he had no time to waste. He cultivated the tutors who could help him the most and these, sensing an exceptional student, were happy to give him time and energy.

It was at the Magical Sciences Centre that Rudge gained access to the long hidden memory cell about King Nikolay. He forced himself to experience again the shame of those long-ago days, analysing his own character as it was at the time, and repeating the analysis over and over until he could find no more new knowledge coming from it. He reviewed his vow of vengeance, and decided that because causing suffering was now one of his main interests, he would continue to pursue Nikolay. He could remember the Ritual of Consolidation into Memory, so he did it again to reinforce the original memory cell. He looked back over the long ago war, and found out in detail just why he had been defeated. First he studied the war from his own point of view, then he switched sides mentally and analysed how Nikolay had been thinking as a strategist and tactician. Analysing Nikolay from a military point of view gave him access to the structure of Nikolay's mental pictures, and from there it was an easy step for Rudge to do a wholesale and complete analysis of Nikolay's mind. He realised that he must do this, because never underestimating his enemy was one of his guidelines and he realised that the knowledge which he had carried over with him from Atlantis, although helpful, would need updating. He focussed on a concave nine-inch diameter mirror made of jet, a kind of magical pre-television screen. The process became easier with practice, and Rudge came to know Nikolay in such detail that he could make accurate guesses about his future. During all this work that Rudge was doing, Nikolay remained happily unaware that his lives were being studied and even, to a certain extent, planned for him. Once somebody knew somebody else as well as that, it was difficult for even a skilled high magician to shake the pursuer off their track. Nikolay was no magician, and only believed vaguely in reincarnation, so he was open and vulnerable to Rudge's machinations. Rudge knew that after all the work he had done, he would meet Nikolay again in physical incarnation sometime between 1850 and 1920 C.E., and Nikolay would fall into his hand like a ripe fruit ready for plucking, consumption and destruction.

Rudge's reputation grew. After twenty years he was invited to join the great Coven of Three Hundred. This is the Outer Court of the Inner Circle of Twelve, the shadowy, hidden Ones who have run the world for thousands of years. Rudge knew he had come home. In his youth he had craved power over individuals and groups. All this was now his, and what he aspired to next, was power over nations.

Rudge stayed at the Centre for another twenty years, consolidating his progress. Then he felt it was time to move. There was no hurry; he was still only seventy. Rigid self-discipline, backed by good tuition and held in place by ambition, would enable him to live for several hundred years.

After discussions, he and his masters decided that he should work his way across the continent, towards the central mountain massifs. On route he was to watch events, practise his trouble-making skills, find recruits, and report to the Centre using astral travel or telepathy, letters being too slow and liable to interference.

By 1550 C.E., Rudge was settled happily in a village a hundred miles south-west of the end of the Hindu Kush mountain range. He had decided to put his feet up for a few months. He was one hundred and fifty years old, but looked forty-five. He bought a house, found labouring work to keep himself going, and melted into the scenery. Some days he sat gossiping among the local men, watching for recruits and studying local politics. After three months, one of the men invited him to come and meet his master. Sensing more than a friendly invitation, Rudge accepted.

Two evenings later, the man led Rudge to a small house outside the village. He served coffee, and disappeared. Rudge sat down in a dim, plain room. Opposite him was a hawk-featured man, head veiled, face greyish brown. Sensing that he was in the presence of a magical superior, Rudge waited.

"I am Isdashir, a humble trader of no particular note." The bland statement alerted Rudge. Isdashir had not invited him here to talk trading. Rudge replied politely, vetting the man's thoughts and aura, sensing whose side he was on. After twenty minutes of platitudes, he relaxed. This man was not a plant, but an ally. Looking satisfied, Isdashir leaned back, stared Rudge in the eye, and smiled for the first time.

"You're right, Brother Rudge. I did not invite you here to talk trading. I was notified by your master at the Centre that you were on your way. During your weeks in my village, I and my manservant have been observing you. I am satisfied and quite impressed. You have correctly noticed that I have certain abilities. Now, I am but a humble servant of those of whom you also are a servant. I have been asked to give you a message, one which will give you a useful lead in your service to those who are our superiors in the great work."

Rudge felt it wise to nod his head in a brief bow. He knew his place. Yes, he had powers, but he also had superiors. Devotees of the work obeyed those above them, or... He focussed on Isdashir.

"I cannot leave this area, because I have to serve here for at least another hundred years. But, Brother Rudge, we are impressed by your progress, and wish to offer you a great opportunity."

Rudge kept his polite expression. So, as he had suspected, Isdashir was one of the Inner Circle of Twelve. He listened even more carefully.

"Our chief agent in Russia is shortly moving to Europe, leaving a vacancy at the Russian court. How do you feel about taking his place?"

Rudge took a deep breath. Even after all his training he was nervous of the august presence facing him. But this vacancy sounded interesting, and he was being offered it by one of the Twelve, those dreaded Ones of whom normal people knew nothing, while exceptional men like himself avoided thinking of them for fear of disturbing the ethers around them. Rudge thought for an instant. Knowing that he dare not refuse, he decided to appear graceful.

"Brother Isdashir, I am grateful for being considered, and accept with full appreciation of the honour you are offering me."

Isdashir's keen expression did not alter. Encouraged, Rudge went on:

"Might I ask the nature of my duties, Brother Isdashir?"

"I cannot say any more now. You already have an excellent grasp of our objectives. I suggest that you start your journey northwards immediately. You must arrive in Moscow not later than one year from now. I will ensure that you are met on route. The man will be a lower grade of operative than you, Brother Rudge, but he will be a former member of the Russian court. He will advise you on recent events, and on procedure and manners. After meeting him you will be better able to formulate your plans in accordance with our wishes for Russia and her people."

The vibrant voice stopped. Rudge realised that he was very cold, and felt dazed. Not since training days had he been weighed in such a merciless balance. It was time to extricate himself.

"I understand, Brother Isdashir. Now, therefore, provided it is your wish, I beg your leave."

"Salutations, Brother Rudge. Work well in your new post, and you will be rewarded."

The manservant was waiting outside. Walking back to the village, Rudge breathed the clean night air with relief, and reflected that his craving for power over nations was nearer to fulfilment.

Some weeks after meeting Brother Isdashir, Rudge was sitting in the highland mountains, resting, his feet propped on a convenient rock. He was several thousand feet above sea level and the thin dry air cut through his clothing. There was a faint perfume, a hint of lying snow, frozen mosses, small cotton grasses, and innumerable tiny flowers. He loved these Central Asian Uplands and their mighty ranges: Kailash, Karakoram, Tien Shan, Hindu Kush, Pamir.

Pamir! This was one of the great geomantic centres of the world. Visiting Mount Pamir was part of his magical education. It meant a detour towards the north-east, but he had plenty of time.

Rudge knew that three powerful Brothers lived around Mount Pamir. Each guarded one of the great rivers of magnetic Earth energy flowing from the depths of the mountain, towards the north, the east, and the south-west. This was done by the Brother tuning in to the energy river, willing it to pass through himself, and putting in it the thought qualities which he knew the Twelve wanted. As the energy river flowed across the landscape just under the surface, the people near it, and their buildings, food and water, were fed with the thoughts of the Twelve. In this way the Twelve kept their dominance, without the people having a clue that they were being controlled.

"That's the way to do it," reflected Rudge. "No need for messy bloodshed or noisy fighting. Keep the lower orders in their place by mental power, and in a few hundred years' time, when the Twelve want to stir them up, the rabble will be used to obeying us and will jump to it when we put loud-mouthed demagogues into their market places."

On a bright autumn morning two days later, Rudge halted twenty miles to the south-west of the peak. He rested, made his mind still, and as a courtesy sent out a thought.

"I am a fellow worker. Greetings! May I visit you?"

Two minutes later he heard the answer in his mind:

"Greetings, fellow worker; please do visit me. I know where you are and am sending out a ray of guidance."

Brother Savidar got next to no visitors, certainly none of his own high magical grade, so he downed tools and welcomed Rudge. The men checked each other with careful questions. Then they relaxed and chatted like old friends, discussing strategy, reviewing progress, and yarning about their youth. Savidar came from the Lueneberg Heath in distant Europe. Short, robust and blond, he was a hundred and ten years old but looked thirty-five. In the luxuriously fitted cave, Rudge rested, and enjoyed the chance to meet an intellectual equal.

On the third afternoon, Savidar invited Rudge to watch an energy processing session. Rudge was very keen. He sat down near the cave mouth, thirty feet from Savidar, and breathed slowly, preparing for three hours of silent watching. He activated his clairvoyant vision, and waited. Savidar, in his linen ritual robes and angular grey felt hat, sat deep in the cave and put himself into a hypnotic trance.

In ancient days the magical masters who originated the work carved out the cave fifty yards from the energy river. A small amount of Earth energy acts like a tonic, but a lot is tiring, so the man had to live near enough to do the work, but outside the core of its magnetic field. Rudge glanced at it through the rock. Like a river of clear water, twenty feet in diameter, coloured deep browns and blues with flecks of silver, it rushed at unguessable speed through the landscape, just below the surface of the ground.

Rudge looked towards Savidar, though not directly at him because attention rays from his eyes would upset the work. He saw Savidar's aura, the magnetic energy field everyone has round them, extend until it was over twenty feet across. The air turned cold. The energy river emerged from the cave wall. Rudge realised that Savidar was drawing it to himself by force of will, and compressing it as it moved through the air towards him. When it reached Savidar it was light grey and a foot in diameter. Savidar reduced his aura to its normal six inches round himself. He held the energy river within it, entering his body below the shoulder blades and leaving through the diaphragm.

Physically quiet but mentally tense, Savidar fed in the thoughts which he knew the Twelve wished. Rudge saw tiny waves bubble up and coloured sparks shine in the energy river. He was fascinated, and was glad he had followed his hunch to visit this Brother who was so steeped in loyalty to the Twelve and their plans. Savidar was forcing conditioning into the energy river as though his life depended on it. Maybe it did, Rudge smiled to himself.

The end was neat. Savidar mentally pushed the energy river away from himself and back to its position in the rock, then watched it to check that it was back to normal. He relaxed for five minutes, looking haggard, then he changed back into everyday clothes, and went out to sit in the sunlight. Rudge stayed where he was. Well trained in energy manipulation himself, he knew that Savidar must be left alone until ready to talk again. Half an hour later, Savidar got up.

"Well now, Brother Rudge, how about a glass or two of my best apricot liqueur?"

Rudge knew he must not mention the work, for this would disturb the energies, which would carry on winding down for four more days.

"Good idea, Brother Savidar, it's an excellent formula isn't it. That spring of yours over there gives fine water."

"It certainly does. It was found by one of the early Brothers, so the tale goes, and has been there for thousands of years. It's full of the magnetic healing powers from the mountain, which is why brothers on my job here have such good health and long lives."

They sat outside the cave and yarned some more, enjoying the evening light.

"Are there any other odd jobs that I can give you a hand with while I'm here, heavy lifting, or anything?" asked Rudge.

"No, thanks a lot, there was only that fallen bit of wall needing fixing. Otherwise I am well set up for winter, with food and fuel ready stacked high, my regular energy work to keep me occupied, and books or my flute for when I take some time off."

"It must get a bit lonely here?" ventured Rudge.

"Can do in winter, but it's not so bad in the warmer seasons, because I can chat to the shepherds I meet when I go for walks; I just make them think I'm one of them and we get on fine. I do look for recruits, but there are not many people at all round here, so there is not much chance to find suitable types for our job. And I'm in regular mental contact with our colleagues at the Centre. No, Brother Rudge, I'm very content with my lot in life."

"And if you weren't you daren't say so," thought Rudge, "because word would get back to your master or even to the Twelve themselves, and you'd be in trouble. Even if I didn't report you, the Assessors of Operative Communications at the Centre would notice."

Out loud he said, "Well, if I could stay for just one more night, I'll be on my way again tomorrow, and thank you so much for all your interesting hospitality, Brother Savidar."

"It's been very good to meet you too, Brother Rudge, and do call in again when you are next at or around Mount Pamir. May our gods bless us both in our endeavours."

Moscow in the late fifteen hundreds was centre of a growing empire and home to thousands of people. Rudge bought a house outside the town, earned his living as a private tutor, and wormed his way into the heart of society. The aims of the mighty Inner Circle of Twelve were always in his mind. He must work to infiltrate into positions of power, incompetents and degenerates who will rule badly, so that the people become poor, and then discontented, and then so desperate that they rebel and tear society apart, burning their own houses and crops. Famine follows, and the starving people look round for a strong man they can lean on. An agent of the Twelve steps out of the shadows and takes over. Rudge's ambition to manipulate nations meshed well with the aims and objects of the Twelve. They knew this, and it was one reason why they had chosen him for the Moscow post.

Periodically, Rudge remembered his desire for revenge against King Nikolay, and one day his aim crystallised: he would set up Nikolay to be a king again, and induce him to destroy his own kingdom. He would not execute him, but keep him alive and let him see it all happen. "Brilliant," decided Rudge. "That's what I'll do to him; I'll really make the stupid bastard suffer."

Rudge had kept himself healthy and knew that barring accidents, he should live six hundred years this time round. That was a decent measure, which he contrasted coldly with seventy years, the life span deserved by common fools, those masses of thoughtless robots whom he despised.

One day, Rudge knew, he would meet again that man whom he knew from thirteen thousand years ago. It would not be for another couple of centuries, but he was busy planning and working, and was content to wait.

Manipulations

In early 1905 Rudge was doing well. The twenty-second of January saw hundreds of Russian people at a peaceful civil rights march shot down by the troops of the emperor, Tsar Nicholas the Second. All round the world, peace-loving, gentle Nicholas was labelled a murderer.

Rudge and Count Christophe Worthton were old enemies, one working against peace, the other for it. Neither was surprised when they met at court in St. Petersburg not long after the disaster. Rudge changed his name and address every ten years to guard against becoming too well known. He was now presenting himself as a Russian nobleman with estates in a far province. He influenced a priest here, an ambassador there, a prince somewhere else. He enjoyed manipulating marriages, mating the criminal with the incompetent to create a manipulatable resource. He was in touch with colleagues overseas, devoted troublemakers, his own recruits. His plans were coming together. Within twenty years Russia would explode. And his masters would note his fine work.

Count Worthton had been working in diplomacy worldwide for many years. No one really knew where he came from, but he liked to pass himself off as north-west European. He was of medium height and build, and looked athletic for his age, apparently about the mid-forties. His face was mid-European with a slight tan, and he looked cultured and intelligent. He liked to dress in good, fashionable clothes, and always wore a gold signet ring with a large diamond which had a family crest engraved on it, although he also sometimes wore a gold watch and chain.

Count Worthton had great respect for Rudge. The two were equal in magical abilities. But the count had one advantage: the Atlantean Pyramid. None of his colleagues around the world needed to know of this tool. It was too important and too dangerous. Only a trained operator could use it. When folded, it looked like a set of table mats. The count kept it in a hollowed-out book in his apartment.

In use, it appeared as a four-sided pyramid with base edges a foot long and a height of nine inches. The sides and base were of whitish quartz a third of an inch thick. The pieces were held together by links of a light yellow metal, similar to steel but with additives unknown since Atlantis, that continent that vanished below the Atlantic Ocean, according to Plato, in about 10,000 BCE. A kidney-shaped ruby, one-and-a-quarter inches by half an inch, formed the main machinery inside. Seven small auxiliary pieces were of quartz. The placing of the pieces governed the role selected, whether thought-power enhancer, long-range viewer, two-way communicator, or psychic spy alarm. It had been dug up in central America by one of the count's ancestors in 500 C.E. and handed down in his family. The count believed and hoped that only one other pyramid of its type now existed. The one he knew of was kept under heavy physical and psychic guard in the depths of the Centre of Magical Sciences, unknown even to staff magicians of the high grade of Rudge.

On meeting at the Russian court one day, the count and Rudge made polite conversation; then they both went off home, to start using both normal and psychic methods to find out what the other was up to.

During his wanderings among the courts of the world, Count Worthton had met many thinkers and mystics. In particular he was impressed by a Siberian, Brother Grigory Efimovich Rasputin-Novykh, a tall, powerful man of insight, strength and discipline. He contacted Brother Grigory, and they discussed their concerns about where Russia was heading. The men agreed that the country was in danger, and decided that Brother Grigory should ingratiate himself into the tsar's court to find out more about who was plotting what, and sabotage the subversion as much as he could. Brother Grigory travelled to St. Petersburg, and settled in the town. By quiet investigation, backed up by good old-fashioned psychic viewing, he discovered that the tsar's son, Alexis, was afflicted by an illness which modern medicine could not cure. Here was his opportunity. He honed up his traditional healing skills, wangled an introduction, and established himself in the imperial court late in 1905.

The Girls

"Don't call me Olly! You're Tatty and I'm going to call you Tatty for ever and ever and ever!"

"If you call me Tatty I'll pull your hair and don't you dare slap me or I'll tell Mamma and Miss Russanova."

"I'll slap you if you pull my hair. Ooh, you'll tear my dress."

"My dear girls, whatever do you think you are up to? Stop arguing this minute, you are a complete disgrace. You remind me of two naughty little boys, rather than grand duchesses of the imperial ruling house."

Olga, ten, and Tatiana, eight, stopped wrestling and stood looking sheepish. In early 1906, the Romanov family and their staff were at Tsarskoe Selo, "Tsar's Village", near St. Petersburg in north-west Russia. To the little girls the splendid palaces and vast estates were simply one of the half dozen homes where they lived with their Mamma and Pappa, sisters and brother, innocently taking it all for granted. Their governess bustled in, all primness and disapproval. She adored the four little girls, but oh dearie me, the way these two elder ones fought each other. She had never met anything like them before.

"Now, girls, apologise to each other please, and we will start lessons."

There was a total silence and two pink little faces glowered up at her.

"Olga, it is your turn to apologise first this time, and I want you to say, 'I'm very sorry, Tatiana, that I called you silly names and pulled your hair.'"

Olga felt furious at the unfairness, because Tatiana had started it all this time, pulling her hair like that and calling her "Olly" when she had been peacefully collecting her books for class. Tatiana ought to apologise first. Olga frowned and blinked, and Miss Russanova waited a bit and then lost patience.

"Go on, Olga. Apologise to your sister, now there's a good girl."

"I'm not going to apologise, please, Miss Russanova."

"Oh, and why not, Olga?"

"Please Miss Russanova, it was Tatiana's fault. She pulled my hair first."

"I did not. Olga pulled my dress and I thought she was going to tear my dress so I pulled her hair so she slapped me and—"

"Please be quiet, Tatiana. Now, listen to me. It doesn't matter who started it, it's both your faults. Olga, you are the elder so you are more responsible, and I want you to apologise first, whether you feel that this particular altercation was your fault or not."

Olga pouted, thinking, how did Miss Russanova always produce unbeatable logic? Oh all right, she'd apologise to Tatiana this time. Still pink and sulky, she said,

"Tatiana, I'm sorry that I called you silly names."

Olga waited to pounce, but Tatiana knew exactly when Miss Russanova's patience would run out so she waited, and then answered just in time.

"Well, in that case, Olga, I'm sorry I spoke rudely to you too."

Miss Russanova pursed her lips.

"Tatiana, it is not for you to pass rash judgement on Olga, so will you please apologise, in the way that you know you should."

To Olga's glee Tatiana looked taken aback.

"Olga, I am sorry for being rude to you and pulling your hair."

Olga was mollified, and Miss Russanova nodded.

"Very good, girls, and no more nonsense please, as from today. So now, let us go to class."

Their sense of fairness satisfied, the two little figures in white frothy dresses, their beautiful reddish hair flowing down over their shoulders, trotted happily along beside their governess on their way to class. Battles forgotten for now, they settled down to lessons.

On a pleasant day early in 1906 Olga and Tatiana sat by the lake shore at Tsarskoe Selo estate with Miss Russanova. The water was dark and still, and Olga thought that she had never seen anything so beautiful. The flat surface seemed to beckon to her, and as she let her mind be drawn towards it she saw a ring of pale mist forming. It filled, forming a pale circle, and cleared, and there in front of her on the water was a map of Mother Russia. Fascinated, Olga wondered, and watched. This was her beloved country being shown to her, the one thing which she cared about above all, so she forgot everything else and studied the map intently as the vision was offered to her.

A big pale cloud spread eastwards from Russia's western borders, slowly across, and stopped just east of the Ural Mountains. It faded, and she felt that it might come back, but it did not. Then a small pale circle appeared just east of the Urals, grew a bit, and faded, and there was only a plain outline again.

The map shook, and Olga frowned to herself, wondering if this meant an earthquake was going to happen. She wished it would stop, but the map went on shaking for what Olga felt was ages although it was really only a minute.

"Earthquakes? Please God, save Russia from an earthquake," she worried to herself, and then she heaved a sigh of relief as the shaking stopped. But things got worse because huge clouds appeared all around the map, and flowed inwards and covered it completely. Stunned, Olga stopped praying and stared, and then she jumped as the map suddenly vanished. She looked round, and saw the lake looking ordinary again, just water and reflections, and to her side were her sister and governess, who did not seem to have noticed anything.

Olga believed in visions, because Mamma and Miss Russanova talked about them, but she thought that only saints had visions, and she was not a saint. Well, this thing which she had seen was a sort of vision, and as she was ordinary, not a saint, maybe this just showed that ordinary girls like her had visions about normal everyday things while saints had visions about holy things; this must be how it worked. Perhaps she should tell Mamma about it, but then, something seemed to tell her very hard not to mention it to her Mamma. She felt so lonely, and longed to tell somebody about it, and then she had a good idea: she would try saying a little to Tatiana later on. Tatiana was an awful bossy-boots, but Olga knew that she could be relied upon to keep quiet about special secrets.

"Right, girls," called Miss Russanova, and Olga jumped again, "We've got another bit of lake to walk around before going back for tea."

"Yes, Miss Russanova," replied the girls, and as Olga stood up she looked again at the water, and sighed, thinking that there were so many things in life which she did not understand and wondering if she would have more insight when she grew up. Over tea Olga was quiet because she wanted to think, and when she saw Tatiana looking at her she hoped that her little sister would not comment in front of Miss Russanova. But her luck held and she had tea in peace.

Later, when she and Tatiana were in bed after lights out, and were supposed to be going to sleep, Olga heard a whisper from across the room.

"Olga."

Olga propped herself up on one elbow.

"Yes, Tatiana?"

"Can I come and talk?"

"Yes of course. What is it?" Tatiana padded over and sat on Olga's bed, wiggling her toes. Olga could see her solemn face dimly in the half dark.

"You were staring at the lake ever so hard today."

"Mmm."

"Were you looking at anything special?"

Olga sat up, and looked closely at Tatiana, wondering whether Tatiana would really keep her secret or just go off and tell tales to Mamma or Miss Russanova. She hesitated, but then her normal sisterly affection and faith came back and she knew she could trust Tatiana.

"I had a vision," she proclaimed.

Tatiana frowned.

"Are you sure, and anyway how do you know it was a vision? Mamma says that only saints have visions, and you're not a saint." She paused for breath. "What did you see?"

Olga sighed, thinking, this was all typical of good old Tatiana, trying to run the entire world, even though she was really quite a nice little sister when she forgot to keep up acting her role of Authority. But Olga knew how to handle Little Miss Bossyboots.

"Tatiana, will you please listen. I did see a vision. It was a map of our Holy Mother Russia, on the surface of the lake, all covered in big huge heavy clouds, and it was shaking a lot and I think there's going to be something awful like a big earthquake in Russia." She frowned at Tatiana, daring her to be rude and say something silly like, what she was saying was all nonsense.

"Olga, what you are saying is all nonsense. Lots of places in Russia don't have earthquakes, and you know that because Miss Russanova said so in class."

"Tatiana, I am not talking nonsense, and I did see a vision on the surface of the lake, of the map of Russia shaking and covered in terrible clouds, and please stop telling me I am talking nonsense because you know that I do not talk nonsense. Stop saying I'm silly. I'm not silly, and you know it. I bet something awful is going to happen to Russia."

"Well, all right, Olga, I'll stop telling you that you are silly, and I agree that what you said sounds interesting. Big clouds over Russia sound bad, and I hope it doesn't mean there's a disaster coming. Did you see anything else?"

"At the beginning there were pale clouds."

"Were there?"

"Yes, but only on the western side of the map, and then they faded out, and I watched for them to come back but they didn't. Also, there was a little pale circular patch, to the eastern side of the Urals, but I didn't know what that meant either. Then at the end there were big storm clouds right over the whole map of Mother Russia, covering it. It was all very strange, but I wasn't frightened and I just sat and watched, and then suddenly the map vanished completely and the lake was ordinary again. What do you think, Tatiana?"

Tatiana was staring at Olga solemnly.

"Well, it certainly all sounds interesting, Olga, but even if you saw a vision of disaster, maybe it won't come true if we all pray hard enough."

"I do hope it doesn't come true, because if it did it would be awful, a great big earthquake and then a storm. I know what I'm going to do, Tatiana: for the next three weeks I'll say extra prayers for Holy Mother Russia every Sunday."

"Yes, that's a good idea," said Tatiana, brightening up. Her big sister became motherly and decided to show who was the elder.

"Look, Tatiana, you'll get cold; you'd better go back to bed."

"Yes, you're right, Olga, goodnight, sleep tight."

Tatiana scrambled down off Olga's bed and went and settled down for the night, but Olga, with passion beyond her years, frowned into the darkness for a long time, worrying about her country and its future.

Conference

In Spring 1906 Count Worthton and Brother Grigory Efimovich Rasputin had one of their rare meetings at the count's apartment in central St. Petersburg. Standing well back from the window, the count looked out to check that no one appeared to be watching from the street. Brother Grigory took his favourite chair. Count Worthton collected the tray of tea prepared by his manservant, settled in his chair, and poured tea for both of them.

"What a pleasure to see you again, Brother Grigory Efimovich. Let us relax and discuss matters."

"Good idea, my esteemed Brother Count Worthton."

"It is almost six months since you arrived at court, Brother Grigory, and I imagine that you are finding it a change from your previous life."

"No, not really, my Brother Count, not so much as you would think. Oh, I know I wear a silk shirt now, instead of plain weave, as it were, but I do find that at heart people are the same wherever they may be. For example, take yourself. You've been to the Holy Land, met people, and travelled widely, even to the Americas, and worked hard in diplomacy all over the world, but you are still the same amiable company that you were when we first met years ago. No, I am very happy here, and now that I have settled in I feel I am fulfilling the role that Almighty God wills for me in helping to support our divinely appointed Emperor in his mighty task of reigning over our great country, God bless her."

"Yet you've met opposition, I hear."

"Yes, Count. Although I cannot effect a permanent cure of His Highness the Tsarevich, it is true that God's power, working through my humble hands, has been known to relieve his affliction on a temporary basis. But some members of the honourable calling of medicine find it hard that I can help the dear child better than they can."

"I receive similar criticism. My wide diplomatic experience, which you kindly mentioned, counts in some gentlemen's eyes as less valuable than university degrees, but then, such is human nature. However, now that you have settled in, do tell me how you are finding the court."

"You wish me to speak frankly, Count?"

"Yes."

"That short-sighted and unwise emperor who many years ago barred women from the succession, has in so doing destroyed the Romanov dynasty."

"Oh? Why?"

"That splendid young woman, Grand Duchess Olga Nicolaeivna, purely because she is a female, is considered unfit to inherit the throne, and so poor Mother Empress has been forced to produce child after child, trying for a male heir, but the result, Alexis, is fatally ill and will not have a long healthy life as emperor anyway. Now, good Mother Empress could and should employ expert help for him, but she trusts no one, fusses around him for hours, and neglects her job of empress, and has reduced the court festivities, which created a lot of much-needed employment and made the people feel that their monarchs cared. Further, she is painfully shy and is using Alexis as her excuse to turn the imperial family inwards behind high walls where she does not need to be seen by her people, many of whom are intensely loyal and are becoming resentful at the imperial family's apparent lack of interest.

"If good Father Emperor was as autocratic as he says he is, he would change that mad, evil ruling and declare Olga his successor. She is a bright girl and would do the job well if trained from youth, but when I suggested it not long ago he roared with laughter, then became angry and accused me of trying to tell him how to run his empire. He should greatly increase court activities, and make the imperial family do its task of providing caring leadership and being a focus for devotion and a light to the nation. But he worships the ground which good Mother Empress walks on, so discontent grows, rumours spread, and I fear a repeat of last year's events."

The count nodded. "I agree with your assessment, but there is still some time to pull the country back from the brink; what do you suggest?"

"I'd like to lock Mother Empress permanently away in a convent and am sorry I can't, but one thing that I am working on is, weaning the emperor off that confounded medicine of his."

"Oh? What medicine?"

"An opium derivative. How it started, was this: in their anxiety to have a son, the imperial couple employed a herbalist, who in his heyday dosed them with every potion imaginable. The emperor became unable to stop, and still quietly gets supplies even though that herbalist has long since left the court, hastened on his way, so the tale goes, by some loyal men who felt he was an undesirable influence. The emperor's large, peaceful blue eyes are famous, but I suspect that a lot of their so attractive peacefulness is due to the infernal mixture to which he has tragically become addicted."

"Dear God in heaven. And the empress?"

"She escaped unscathed, and subsequent to my investigations I am sure she knows of the emperor's problem, but I can't understand why she doesn't help him beat it unless perhaps she believes the country doesn't need him while she is there to rule in his place."

Brother Grigory paused. "There is however a more sinister possibility, my Brother Count, and therefore, may I continue to speak man to man, in absolute and permanent confidence?"

"Please do, Brother Grigory."

"The empress has fallen into the hands of devil worshippers, my Brother Count."

"I have heard these stories, Brother Grigory, but I am perturbed to hear them from you. Do go on."

"In her desperation to produce a son, the empress turned not only to the herbalists but also to anti-religious practices, and wrongly blaming herself for the plight of her much-treasured son, fell further and further into the hands of practitioners of the left-hand path. It is said that she went so far as to make a pact with the evil one in return for a son, but the evil one, being the father of lies, deceived her in that the son he gave is ill and will not live to rule Russia anyway. Even while losing her soul to the evil one, the empress has also lost all benefit from the arrangement, and has so got herself into the grip of evil forces that no ordinary priest could help her, in fact, no one can help her at all unless and until she herself makes the first move, and that is unlikely. Unable to extricate herself from those men's grip, she keeps up her wicked practices, trying to get Alexis cured. She has lost everything, gained nothing, and undermined the imperial family more than did even her most wicked or unwise forebears. Our country is under the control of those who control the empress, and is falling into the abyss. This may all sound preposterous, but it is what I have observed since arriving at court."

"You are sure that this is all true, Brother Grigory?"

"Count, why do you think so many rumours surround the imperial couple, and why do we continually witness the inexplicable dismissals of competent men of the court? I am as sure as anyone can be."

"Does the empress work alone?"

"No. She is a member of one of the many clandestine and magical groups that are rotting the court."

"Who are the others in her group?"

"Six members of the imperial family, three senior military officers, two medical men and myself."

"So you managed to become a member; that's good."

"Yes, Count. I demonstrated various magical skills, to quite a high standard I must say, and after about six weeks, during which I know that other investigations were being made about me and I was heavily spied upon, I was admitted early this year."

"What sort of rituals have you witnessed the empress taking part in?"

"Firstly, the 'rite of power'. You know, Count, the details of this ritual?"

"Yes. During my training I had to study such things, unfortunately."

"Also, every month just before the new moon they, or perhaps I should say we, practise a ritual that generates protection for the group and its work. And we do other work too of course, aimed at such things as keeping power in the hands of the few and using the masses of the people as our mental and physical menials."

"You are implying that the emperor does not take part?"

"No. Not only am I sure he does not know that the group exists, but I believe that if he was told of it and even shown proof he would simply refuse to believe it. The emperor has many fine qualities, he is cultured and compassionate, and strives for national and international peace, but he is, with the greatest of respect, too good, and as a result is unable to see the evil around him. Alas for holy monarchs, they are hardly ever truly effective. You can see, I feel, why it suits the empress's controllers to keep him on opium. I do of course realise that in some societies it is considered socially normal and acceptable to smoke a regular pipe of these infernal mixtures, but this does not alter the fact that once having started, most people find it hard to stop."

"Does the empress have other aims in her magic besides her son's health?"

"No. She thinks that she has freedom of thought in her running, as she calls it, of Russia and its empire, but in fact, two members of the group, a military man and a doctor, run her. These two work under another man, known by various names and seldom seen at court, whom you may know of; I think his original name is Baron Verion Rudge, but he appears and disappears under different names over the years."

"Oh, yes, Rudge; I know him from many decades ago. If he is one of the main subversives we are fighting, you and I, Brother Grigory Efimovich, are going to have a hard and a long fight. So he is not a member of the empress's group?"

"No. He may be a member of one of the others, but after quiet investigation I haven't found any sign of it, and I assume he is most interested in the empress's group. Rudge, as you already appear to know, is one of the world's greatest evil magicians, and a man of his degree can exercise as much influence as he wishes while remaining at a distance. His agents control everything the empress does and, through her, the empire. They do what they want, when they want, and have all the material wealth they need to accomplish their aims. They are some of the most perverted and direly twisted men I have ever met, and that's saying something."

"But, Brother, what do they actually aim to do in this country, and why?"

"I'll deal with why first. Why, is the sheer pleasure of seeing people suffer. We have to face facts, and as you already know, my Brother Count, there are forces, not just in this world but running this world, who are intent on causing suffering, not just for an odd individual here or there, but for twenty millions of people at a time."

"I'm afraid you are right, Brother Grigory."

"And they intend no other than mass social upheaval here in Russia. Believe it or not, I recently heard one of them call last year's events 'a rehearsal for the real thing'. They aim to disrupt Russia, install a dictatorship far worse than even the present well-meaning but inept regime, and then to spread their system through country after country. Their final aim is a dictatorship of the evil one over the entire world, to be accomplished by the year two thousand Common Era."

The men sat thinking. Count Worthton got up and walked round the room, his senses alert.

"No one listening in, Brother Count?"

"I don't think so, but we can't be too careful. As my old master used to put it, 'Beware of ears that flap unseen', and operatives of the grade of Rudge and his pack are not repelled by nicely perfumed flowers or clichés about love and peace. Let me think, will you excuse me for quarter of an hour?"

"Certainly."

Count Worthton took from the shelf a heavy leather-bound book, went into the next room, and closed the door behind him. He went to a bureau, and moved it round so that sitting at it, he would face south, as he preferred for psychic viewing. He opened the bureau, put the book down and unlocked it, took out the Atlantean pyramid, and put the book away. It took him two-and-a-half minutes to set up the pyramid. He sat down and did a minute's deep breathing, then stared at the sloping triangular plate facing him.

Round the centre of the plate a patch six inches across turned opaque white. He waited. The patch turned silver, ready for his mental instructions. He willed his study to appear, and saw himself pictured, a tiny, still figure, surrounded by bookshelves in the familiar room.

He willed distance, and the study vanished towards the centre of the picture, while the salon appeared. He saw Brother Grigory Efimovich, taking tea. The pictures appeared at the edge, then folded inwards one after the other, growing smaller and vanishing at the centre of the picture. He kept this up until he got a picture of the apartment block seen from across the street, and willed this to stay on the triangular plate, now a viewing screen. Then he went searching. He altered the vibration of his brain waves up and down the spectrum, checking a wide band of frequencies, and then at last he found a trace, which he knew must be Rudge. On the bottom left hand corner of the screen he saw the back of the familiar head and shoulders, hovering in the air, looking towards the apartment block. He did not try to read his enemy's thoughts because he knew that even when he was using the pyramid, with its built-in filtration, any telepathic probing might alert Rudge.

Count Worthton noted that his enemy was on the job; then he closed the viewing session. He quietly said three words in the ancient, very dangerous Atlantean priestly language, words whose sound would kill an untrained user. The picture faded, and then he went and sat at the far side of the room, eyeing the pyramid as he sipped water. He went back to the pyramid, waved his hands round it to check that the magnetism created by his brain waves had dispersed, and then folded it and locked it back in the hollowed-out book. The whole process had taken eighteen minutes. He went back into the salon and replaced the book on the shelf. Brother Grigory was sitting peacefully. Count Worthton sat down and poured tea.

"It's as we thought. Our old friend Baron Rudge is trying to watch, but I'm keeping him at bay with the barrier I always put up round the apartment during discussions. But to return to what you were saying about his henchmen and their aim to destroy Russia. You are based at the court, working from the inside to foil them, but you are isolated, with no others whom you can trust."

Brother Grigory shook his head.

"For me, trusting is not an option. I know well what my fate would be if the others in the group found me out, and I trust only you. It is true that I have plenty to do. I want to get his imperial majesty off that mixture, possibly backing up persuasive words with some mild hypnotism, and secondly, push him to assert his authority more. Thirdly, I aim to stop the rot being spread by the magical and political groups, the empress's one in particular. I must not be seen talking to you at court, but what about meeting here in four weeks' time at, say, three o'clock?"

The count consulted his diary.

"Yes, that would be convenient to me."

"Brother Count, may I ask you a blunt question?"

"Yes."

"For whom are you working: yourself, or a group, and if a group, who?"

"I am one of a small band of men and women from all countries, who work behind the scenes. We wish to save mankind from suffering, and we help as much as we can, but what we can do is limited, and we suffer much frustration due to the great power of the opposition, who continually sabotage our work. As you know, the only real sin on Earth is ignorance and all others flow from that, so we soldier on, sometimes feeling futile but always hoping and praying that more people will see the light and turn back to the universal Laws of God. When enough people do this, the necessity for suffering on Earth will stop, and we will no longer be needed to help save humanity from its own deliberate stupidity.

"However, Brother Grigory, you are living here now and you see the emperor more than I do. You are having a wholesome influence on their majesties and are getting me much useful information. I am up to date now and look forward to our next meeting, so do look after yourself until then."

"I certainly will, my esteemed Brother Count, and may God bless you. Good afternoon."

Audience

Many people tried to persuade Tsar Nicholas to grant the Russian people a better measure of modern rights, but it was a slow process. In September 1906 Count Worthton returned from travels overseas where he was helping a civil rights group, and Brother Grigory Efimovich updated him on events in St. Petersburg, where progress was lethally slow. The two men applied for an audience, and the tsar consented to see them.

"Maybe letting them talk will get them off my back," he thought. "They're an arrogant pair of ill-mannered ignoramuses, always coming in here and telling me how to run my empire."

He accepted their formal bows with pretended grace which did not fool any of them, and the three men got down to business.

Count Worthton started by begging the tsar to grant the people more civil rights. Nicholas had heard similar pleas before, but it did not sink in this time either. At the words "civil rights", Nicholas labelled any speaker, even the count, a dangerous subversive, and stopped listening. Brother Grigory backed up the count but it was hard going. Nicholas hedged.

"But, my dear Count, I do believe that I should consult my wife on this." He lounged back in his chair, legs stretched out. Count Worthton looked frosty; he did not like being called "dear".

"Sir," went on the count, "last year you had that terrible revolution, when your monarchy was threatened and almost fell. Do you not think you should be altering your methods of ruling?"

Nicholas looked half-asleep. He gazed into space, frowning. Count Worthton and Brother Grigory glanced at each other and waited patiently. They understood Nicholas. Eventually the emperor stirred.

"Well, you see, my dear Count, I cannot change anything," the other two felt incredulous but kept their polite expressions in place, "because I am an autocratic ruler. As you know, when I succeeded to the throne I promised to uphold the traditional methods of ruling Russia and all her lands. I cannot change."

"Even if your methods have already led to one nearly fatal disturbance, sir?"

"No. I cannot change the way I rule. My wife," he broke off in time not to say, "My wife won't let me." Count Worthton and Brother Grigory stared hard at him, realising what he had been going to say, but Nicholas sat oblivious, not noticing that they knew.

"My wife doesn't think it is a good idea."

"Sir, you are the ruler, not your noble lady wife."

"I know. But…" a few seconds' silence, "my wife helps me with the weighty task of ruling my empire, and I listen to her views because I have always found them helpful."

Count Worthton took a deep breath and leaned forward in his chair, feeling that despite his vast diplomatic experience, he was glad Brother Grigory was there backing him up. Men had gone to the salt mines in Siberia for disagreeing with tsars, but Russia herself was dying, and impelled by that awful thought he decided to persevere further.

"Sir, I repeat. You are the emperor, not your noble lady wife. I do not contest your right to choose the counsellors you wish. But may I respectfully remind your imperial majesty that there are in your court men who have travelled the world and have experience and knowledge of international affairs which your lady wife, no matter how spiritual or nobly intentioned, does not have. I submit, Sir, that this realm could be better served if counsellors were employed who were of, shall I say, a more conventional background."

"You do not understand me, my dear Count. My wife's advice is essential to me. We share a spiritual vision and questing which is peculiar to us and I consider my lady wife a full partner in the sacred task placed on me by Almighty God, that of ruling this my great Russian empire."

"Sir, with all due respect to you, it is obvious to an observer that your methods of ruling, if not changed, are going to lead your empire into worse turmoil than that which they produced last year."

Nicholas jumped up furiously. "How can you say that?"

"Sir, after eleven years of your rule, a great mass of your people came to your capital city asking you, sir, for freedom and rights. Not only were you absent, which they saw as running away, but your soldiers fired on them, on men, women, and children, who were walking in an orderly manner along the streets of your city, singing hymns and invoking The Names of God and of His Saints.

"Sir, this cannot go on. Change has got to be brought about, or another explosion, worse than that one, will blow your empire into irreparable pieces.

"Forgive me, Sir, for being so blunt."

Nicholas had sat down. He looked stunned.

"But do you not see, my dear Count, those marchers were not my loyal populace. They were a minority led by rabble-rousers, by those accursed socialists. They were putty in the hands of those who wish to destroy the empire. My real people love me and accept my rule."

"Sir, surely a hundred thousand people is more than a mere minority, and is a number worthy to be heard by you, their 'Little Father under God'?"

"No, they are not worthy to be heard, and neither are they worthy of anything. My dear Count, you do not understand me, nor my wife, nor my empire. Do you not see that I am their absolute ruler and emperor? I rule them, and in return, they give me their trust and loyalty. Those people who marched, no matter how many, are not the true people of my empire."

"Sir, why do you think they marched?"

"Because, as I have just told you, my dear Count, they were misled by evil agitators behind the scenes."

"Sir, many of those people who marched last year, travelled far, and suffered severe privations to save money for their expenses out of the pittances which they earn. Therefore do you not think, Sir, that more was inspiring them than the words of agitators?"

"It is not my fault if those men earn a pittance. They should work harder, or find other employments."

"The facts remain, Sir, that most of them earn little, and they gave up time and money they could not afford to come and march peacefully, singing hymns, to implore you, their emperor, to give them freedom and civil rights. Sir, they trusted you."

"And rightly so. Am I not their Little Father under God?"

"Sir. Brother Grigory Efimovich and I sought audience with you today, to implore you to give your people an enhancement of freedom and civil liberties. They are crying out for this throughout your empire. Do you refuse all their prayers?"

"My dear Count, I have granted both of you my time and been patient with you. My answer is a firm No. My people are MY people, and my true subjects are contented and loyal."

He stood up and, turning his back on them, strolled across to the window and stared outside. The two visitors realised that the emperor was ending their audience, and gave up. They bowed themselves out. Nicholas sat down again and sat frowning and sulking.

"Don't my dear friends see that as an autocratic monarch I cannot allow my people to start ruling themselves? The idea is ridiculous. What can farmers and miners and gardeners know about ruling? They have not been trained in it. I am trained in ruling, therefore I rule. I do not set out to farm or mine just because I wish to. Every man performs the task ordained for him by Almighty God, and in this way, society remains stable and orderly."

The Vision in the Garden

Olga, being the eldest, felt protective and motherly towards her little sisters. Until she got older and realised that no two people are the same, she was puzzled because the three "babies" were so different from each other. But later she understood, and became a natural teacher, learning what they were each like and encouraging them.

Her relationship with the youngest in the family, her brother Alexis, was different and complex. All the girls loved him, but from his birth, when she was almost nine, Olga knew he was what her parents had been waiting, longing and praying for, and that they thought her a second-class citizen because she was a girl. She could not help her motherly heart going out to this chubby little baby and wrapping him up safely in the warmth of her love, but at other times she would remember and rebel, feeling the injustice angrily. "Why will that fifth in line child have the throne and privileges I should have? I am the eldest, the First Born; he isn't!"

One spring day in 1907 she was in a really bad mood. The imperial family were at their home in the Crimea, and the children were playing with their nurse and governess in the big fenced garden. By the gate a group of guard soldiers hefted their weapons, gossiped, and passed an unofficial cigarette round. The day was warm and humid, the women were tired in their heavy dresses, and even the trees drooped. Most comfortable were the four girls in the light frocks that their mother the Empress liked.

Tatiana, Marie and Anastasia were playing with Alexis. Olga had gone off on her own. She was sitting on the grass, which needed cutting, leaning on the knobbly wooden fence, which needed cleaning. She knew that her dress would pick up dirty marks, but she was in the mood for a battle with her mother. She glowered across at the others, thinking furious thoughts about her usually much loved brother. "Alexis in the bright light and me in the shade, that's how things always are for us, little twat, throne-stealer, sod him." She enjoyed trying out the new rude words she had overheard from the soldiers, then she wriggled and turned pink, afraid that their governess could hear her naughty thoughts.

In a minute Miss Russanova would call out to ask her why she was sitting over there on her own. To avoid a silly questioning session followed by an even sillier sermon of clichés, she must rejoin the others. "Just another minute's peace, please, God, before I have to go and pretend to be good," she thought, staring at Alexis resignedly. Then everything in her life changed for the second time as her latent psychic ability, guided by her Holy Guardian Angel, switched itself again into activation.

The garden faded, as a giant grey screen, eight feet tall and fifteen feet wide, appeared, hanging in the air six feet in front of her. Alexis appeared, a moving monochrome picture, smart and adult in an army uniform but dreadfully thin and gaunt, looking around him as though hunting for something lost. Olga knew intuitively that he was aged fourteen, and then she held her breath while the screen hung there.

The picture of Alexis faded, and next she saw a chair, one of the big ornate ceremonial thrones which she loved looking at, with its lavish cloths and gold decorations. It was empty, and she waited, confident that Pappa's picture would appear and fill it up and show it the way it ought to be, with Pappa firmly ruling Russia as emperor, as he always would for ever and ever.

But she waited, and waited.

And then she realised that she was cold, feeling a sort of inside coldness she had never felt before, coming from under her heart, and spreading through her until after a few seconds she was one little block of solid ice. Then she knew that the coldness was fear, and she was seeing her country's future. The words 'downfall of the monarchy' were too big for her, but into her head came the knowledge that the throne Pappa sat on so splendidly now, would one day be empty.

The vision faded, and she saw the untidy grass, the groups of people, the trees and the sky.

She stared at the others, feeling a jolt at how normal they all looked. Miss Russanova was pointing at something in a book Marie was frowning over, and Olga wondered if any of them had noticed her staring into the air at nothing. Just then, Tatiana looked up and fixed Olga with a sharp look. Olga stared back. Tatiana's firm expression brought her back to reality and with relief she got up, walked over, sat down by Tatiana and took her hand.

"So, what's going on with you then, sister?" asked Tatiana quietly.

"Erm, nothing much," Olga mumbled. Then she whispered, "I'll tell you tonight, after lights out. I saw something awfully funny, in the air, it was on a screen like a film, about Pappa and Alexis."

Then she stopped, because Miss Russanova did not like her pupils whispering. Olga knew the cliché off by heart. "Talk to the whole company, or do not talk at all. Nice girls speak clearly, naughty girls mumble and you can't hear them at all."

Olga sighed. Even at that young age, she knew she was too obedient. She was afraid to be brave like Tatiana. She felt deeply that if she defied Miss Russanova or her parents, the whole universe would explode, or implode, or Pappa would drop dead, or something awful. It was not fair. If Tatiana had rampaged about, defying governesses and nurses, she would get a totally different reaction, but Tatiana wouldn't rampage about, because she was too dignified. Olga wouldn't rampage, because she knew that she would feel bad about it later, and the self-criticism was the worst punishment of all, far worse than a telling off or extra lines. She was beginning to taste the awful loneliness of the person who cares with devastating intensity about something which most other people do not care or even think about.

Wishing she could be different, Olga pretended to join in with the other children, but she felt strange, a sort of horrible fated feeling which never left her from then on for the whole of the rest of her life.

She stared across to the place where she had been sitting by the fence.

For a few seconds, a second vision for that day came to her. She was looking down a tunnel which opened up in front of her, its sides a swirl of pale cream coloured light. And at the other end of it was a young woman aged twenty-one, staring down through the tunnel at her. It was herself, looking back in time at young Olga in the garden. The little girl stared at the young woman, wanting to learn all that she could of her own future. But all she could see was greyness, deprivation, and the clouds of war. She blinked in concern, wondering if she could be wrong but somehow knowing with absolute certainly that the vision was true. And the eyes of the vision! They were full of sorrow and despair, and had seen horrible things which little Olga did not yet know or understand. Then this vision, also, faded, slowly, and the eyes of the young woman haunted the little girl until they disappeared last.

Conversation, 1908

One day in spring 1908 the imperial family and a couple of close relations were seated at luncheon at Tsarskoe Selo. Olga loved this room. The high ceiling stretched away forever, the walls had some of her favourite plasterwork of cherubs and leaves, and the curtains were over thirty feet long. Olga was twelve, and very conscious of her dignity, with her round face, lovely clouds of reddish hair, and solemn expression. When the conversation around the table reached a suitable juncture she took a couple of deep breaths, screwed up her courage, and plunged in to what had been infuriating her for nearly all her life.

"Pappa," she said, "I'm the oldest, not Alexis. Why can't I have the throne of Russia when I grow up?"

Everybody stared, except Tatiana, who had discussed the subject with Olga several times and knew that Olga planned to raise it with their parents. Olga had declared that even if the answer were "No!", she wanted to know she had tried to obtain the throne and save Russia from disaster.

Her father Tsar Nicholas looked at Olga, then across at Alexandra, and smiled as he looked back at Olga. She was intent, barely breathing, waiting for his answer and totally conscious that this was one of the most important moments in her whole life. Her heart sank as she saw his amused leer, and she realised he was too thick and arrogant to take her seriously. Resigned and in despair, she waited for the sexist putdown.

"My dear Olga, you know very well that women cannot inherit the throne of Russia." The exact words Miss Russanova had used last week. No respect, no civility, just contempt. "Why do I bother?" thought Olga. "Bloody grown-ups are all the same. And why the hell does he say 'dear' when he only uses it as an insult. If he really thought I was as dear as all that, he would listen to me properly."

"I know, Pappa, but why not?" she said out loud.

"Your ancestor the late Tsar Paul instituted the rule many years ago."

"I know, Pappa. But it's not fair. You could change the rule so that I can. Look at all the good empresses that there have been throughout history, and queens too, like our great and noble Catherine, and that marvellous Elizabeth in England, and the Judge Deborah, a wonderful soldier, and the Queen of Sheba, and Queen Esther in the Bible." Amazed at her own boldness, she dredged her mind for every example she could think of, and went on talking until she had run out of breath.

"Olga, you know that it is impossible. I swore to hand to my successor everything I have received from my late royal father. Therefore, I cannot change the rule banning women from the throne of the Russian Empire."

Olga had heard it all so many times before. Banging her head against a brick wall would have been easier than trying to argue her way to the throne. And why couldn't Pappa change the rule? He said he was an absolute ruler, so surely that meant he could institute a change to the constitution if he felt like it? The power her parents wielded made her feel sick. She doubted that it would be any use saying any more because even if she brought up some new and original argument, Pappa would just repeat his so-called logic like a robot. Please God, help her to help Russia. But without the throne, how could she help Russia?

Then, to Olga's surprise and horror, her mother went on the attack.

"Olga, you are a presumptuous child, full of naughtiness. How dare you speak to your father like that? He is Emperor of All The Russias, and his word is law to his one hundred and thirty million subjects, all of whom love him and kneel reverently at his feet. How can you, insignificant, unimportant and arrogant child, set yourself above him, arguing when he speaks from his imperial authority? Apologise now or I will punish you most severely."

The unfairness staggered Olga and for a blissful moment anger and pure hatred for her mother and her father seethed within her, but then her old familiar failing of obedience let her down and her shoulders slumped as she felt herself slide into the old servile mindset. She despised herself as even again she knew that due to her own stupidity and uselessness Russia was doomed, and she dared not even argue any more with her father.

Her face distorted with contempt for both herself and her father as she invented a nice cringeing apology, thinking to herself, "We're as bad as each other; he is in the position to rule and can't do the job, and I could do the job but can't get into the position to do so."

"I'm very sorry for what I said, Pappa."

Nicholas looked at Alexandra.

"He's asking her for instructions," thought Olga, "or why doesn't he answer me himself?"

"Olga," snapped Alexandra.

Olga looked at her mother, and was hit by a look on Alexandra's face which she had never before seen, a suspicious, intent expression.

And those eyes, what colour were they, blue, grey, or, what was happening, were they orange, because the colour shifted so fast that Olga could not keep up. Now there was a terrible pain in the middle of her forehead and the dining room and the people vanished, and all she could see was eyes, orange, penetrating eyes. Mamma's eyes. But they couldn't be; Mamma's eyes were loving soothing blue-grey, and gentle, but these eyes were a Devil's eyes. "Mamma! Help me! Where are you?" Olga's mind said in a bewildered prayer, but Mamma was not there. A crackling noise blew through Olga's head and the pain stopped, leaving only a clamminess. Olga could see the dining room again and Mamma was there sitting at the table, looking normal with her bluish-grey eyes and beautiful, familiar face.

What had happened? Had anything happened? Olga could not remember; she only knew that she had been frightened of eyes. But Mamma's eyes were expressionless. Olga glanced into them, then tried to look away but couldn't, and tried again and couldn't. Some part of her thoughts said, "Please God, help," and instantly there was a sound inside her forehead like taut rubber snapping. Olga blinked, feeling released. She did not know what she had been released from, but the freedom felt wonderful.

"Olga." Olga heard her mother's voice but did not want to look up at her, and stared at the table, feeling frightened of her mother's gaze although she did not know why.

"Olga, please look at me when your mother is speaking to you," said Alexandra. From the other corner of her eye Olga saw Nicholas shift uneasily. She did not want to look at Alexandra, but she could not save herself and the room vanished and all that existed was one all-engulfing orange eye while sensation stopped and real life was somewhere else. She was falling into that huge eye. Obedient, obedient, obedient! The word thundered through her head like a nightmare drumbeat out of hell. Olga had to be obedient to Mamma's will. Only Mamma's orange eye existed and it was the universe and Olga had to surrender herself into it.

Crash! Olga jumped as Tatiana's knife clattered accidentally against a plate, but the noise saved her by stirring her from the trance, and once more she was able to look round normally at the people and the room. She felt drawn to glance at her mother, and wondered why Mamma's face was tight with anger, frowning down at the table. Funny, there was a gap in her mind, or was there? Surely she had just been thinking about something really important, but then, if the thing had been important, she would remember it automatically, wouldn't she?

Olga carried on with her lunch. She noticed Tatiana was observing her, but that was normal. Dear old Tattikins loved policing the three of them but all the same, she was staring what looked like especially hard this time. Olga decided she would ask her why later, but she forgot about it, and somehow the incident slipped Tatiana's mind too.

Woodland Thoughts

Olga was standing in a wood at Tsarskoe Selo, deep in early spring greenness. Under her feet was flat mossy earth, with broken twigs and new shoots. Above her head floated the branches of thick old deciduous trees, just coming into leaf, and a cool breeze, with a breathy sound, stirred the small branches.

Olga felt incredibly aware. Engrossed in a mild state of nature contemplation, she saw time lines going out from herself in all directions. It was one of those moments remembered through many lives. The party of three, Olga, Tatiana, and Emperor Nicholas, stood and looked in silence, wanting to preserve the moment, while their carriage driver whispered to the patient horses and their guard troop of mounted soldiers looked at the familiar scenery with resigned boredom.

Olga loved the beauty, but it meant little to her. Although only fifteen years old she was politically adult, and she was consumed with worry. She could feel something wrong with her country, something like evil human worms, insidious creatures of secrecy, eating the foundations of all she loved. And that man over there, her emperor, did not know anything about it.

"How can he be so ignorant?" she asked herself. "I can see the end approaching for Russia and I have got ideas about how to prevent it. But Pappa is sleepwalking towards disaster and taking his country with him. Tatiana and I try to discuss it with him, but he takes no notice. He ignores us because we are his own daughters, which doesn't say much for how he brought us up. I don't love him any more. How can I love an emperor who can't see the coming destruction of the country he rules?

"I'd consult Tatiana again, but we don't get on when we're discussing Russia. She is very wise in spiritual things, but she can't tune in to the hidden factors which affect Russia's wellbeing. I have always been able to feel our country's soul in a way that she can't. When we discuss it, and I say I think the country would be better off with a forceful leader not a holy one, she gets furious because I've dared to criticise Pappa, and she misses the whole point of what I'm trying to say. Oh, blow it and blow her. She never comes up with ideas anyway. I'm not going to bother with trying to talk to her any more about it all.

"It's so beautiful here. All Russia is beautiful, with her forests, fields, plains, mountains, seas, deserts, marshes, rivers, orchards, and secret hidden places. She is the biggest realm in the world, and I think the most wonderful. If only I could look forward to being empress, but it's pointless going over that again!"

Olga thought her way through her favourite prayers and psalms, but they did not help her to feel better.

"Prayers alone don't work," she realised. "It's prayers plus action that Russia needs, and she certainly won't get the required action, promptly enough, from dear old Pappa. What CAN I do? Kill him and Mamma and Alexis, and bag the throne? But plotters need accomplices and I can't do it alone. People are loyal to them so I'd only get killed if I did anything on my own, and that wouldn't help Russia.

"It's funny, isn't it. Here I am, standing here aged fifteen and looking innocent, while thinking calmly about murdering half my family; but it wouldn't be murder if it was judicial execution, done to save my people from catastrophe. Maybe it counts morally as being on the same level as killing the enemy in a just war. I'll have to think about that as I don't want to displease Almighty God, well, not too much anyway.

"Thank goodness Tatiana and I are soon going to meet Count Worthton for further instruction in advanced diplomacy. I do hope we can speak freely to him and not just utter polite clichés. When Pappa told us he had planned the meeting, I hoped it might mean that he was taking me seriously as heir should Alexis die, but no such luck. Still, I'm going to learn all I can, because if I am trained and prepared, the chance to serve my country might come sooner or later."

Nicholas looked at his watch.

"Well, it's lovely here, ladies, but it is time to start returning home. We have all got duties or classes to get back to, haven't we."

"Yes, Pappa," the girls nodded politely, and Olga stared around again at the tremendous, vibrant woodland beauty, feeling cut off from it by the deep nagging despair about Russia's future that was her constant unspoken nightmare companion. She joined her father and sister as they trooped back to the carriage and climbed in.

A Walk With Brother Grigory Efimovich

As Olga and Tatiana got older, Empress Alexandra allowed them out for chaperoned walks with Brother Grigory Efimovich. By now Olga was sixteen and Tatiana fifteen, and they liked the way he treated them as intelligent adults.

Brother Grigory used to lead the little group across the sweeping lawns, always Olga to his left and Tatiana to his right, and then he would start talking. He was a great talker. For forty minutes he steered the enchanted girls all round the big lake and back again. The girls did "Nature Study" in class, but when it came to real deep study of nature, Brother Grigory was in a category of his own.

One day, he was talking about the birds, and the girls listened spellbound as he described the huge white herons.

"They are marvellous water creatures," he said, "always moving about their nests in the breeding season to keep the young birds safe. You see, the young are prey to lots of things, such as fish that jump out of the water to catch them, and animals that lurk in the reeds and reach into their nests to catch them and take them for their own families of young to eat."

Olga giggled, not really believing him.

"Oh, Brother Grigory," she disagreed bravely, "Surely there aren't fish that can really jump out of the water as far as a bird's nest and catch the young ones," but he assured her that some fish did do.

"The animals, birds and fish in Siberia have to be very aggressive, and catch lots of food quickly, so as to put on the large amounts of weight that they need to survive the winter," he explained, "That's why some of the things they do to get food seem unbelievable."

Olga thought about this, and nodded, while Tatiana was busily storing everything away in that brain of hers. Sometimes the other three girls felt as though she was a one-woman filing system, memorising everything so as to catch them out later, preferably in front of their parents.

Brother Grigory went on, "My dear and respected ladies, here in St. Petersburg you have never seen anything like those huge herons. Their wingspan is enormous, over seven feet. They are immensely strong, with huge beaks three feet long, like a battering ram and very sharp. One of them could fight a big man and kill him, and indeed this did happen once, in a village near mine. And the way that they like to stand still, while they wait for fish to come near to them, is phenomenal. No saint, meditating on the Lord God in a church in St. Petersburg, was ever more silent and unmoving than those great birds, wonderful works of God's holy world."

Brother Grigory nodded slowly and made the Sign of the Cross on himself. Olga and Tatiana followed his example, and waited for their holy man to speak, not dreaming of interrupting what they saw as his pious thoughts. He charmed the Romanov children, with his talk about God and the Saints on one hand, and the wonders of His World of Creation on the other.

Their parents kept the family isolated to protect Alexis, who was ill. If they had had a normal social life, they could have had such fun, meeting other girls from local families, and then, in later years, going to respectable upper-class social events with carefully selected young men. But the girls did not get out as much as they would have liked, so their meetings with Brother Grigory helped to broaden their outlook.

He particularly helped Olga, because her self-respect was always under threat from Tatiana. Even though the two elder girls were devoted to each other, Olga found Tatiana trying at times, especially because Tatiana was growing taller and got taken for the eldest, which was shattering and annoyed Olga almost more than anything. The worst thing was, Tatiana was Mummy's Girl. Olga detested Mummies' girls, even though her conscience was flexible enough not to mind that she herself was Daddy's Girl. She would sometimes sit and sulk to herself, "I don't like Tatiana because she is Mummy's Girl, but I do love Tatiana because she is wonderful and brave and holy." The respect Brother Grigory gave her because she was the eldest cheered her up.

The walks with Brother Grigory were some of the best times of Olga's youth. Olga adored the link he provided with a wider and more natural life. When she felt the wind move her hair, she had blissful secret visions of living in Siberia, catching fish and birds to eat, finding plants and mushrooms, building a hut from branches, and even weaving goats' hair to make herself a cloak.

But Olga had enough decency to know that she herself was in a fortunate minority in having material comfort. She had intense curiosity about all the Russians, whom she regarded as 'her people' even though she realised she would never rule them as their empress as she longed to, and it was Brother Grigory who told her and Tatiana about the millions of forgotten and destitute citizens who lived outside the walls of her own luxurious homes. Secretly, she was a bit of a socialist. She had sympathy for the section of society whom she thought of as "those poor people", but enough sense not to wish that she were one of them. Really poor people, she realised, were so busy trying to survive that they could not help themselves much, and a person who was rich could do more to create the improvements in society which would help worse off people to raise themselves. If she couldn't become empress, she often thought, she wouldn't have minded having an ordinary job, like one of their governesses. The thought of being married off as a beautiful pawn in a political arrangement horrified her, and even though she felt reassured by her father's declarations that he would never force any of his daughters into a marriage for his own political reasons, she still felt fearful that her own sense of patriotic duty might do this sort of forcing, and push her into a marriage which she knew would give her a lifetime of unhappiness, out of some obscure guilt-addled wish to serve Russia, almost, by being unhappy if she couldn't be empress. Not for the first time, she realised that material wealth and high position can have their own disadvantages.

One Day in 1912

One day Olga came up to Tatiana at Tsarskoe Selo, and the girls greeted each other, then Olga said,

"And do you know, Tatiana, this morning I met Brother Grigory Efimovich in the corridor leading to the library. He was singing ever such a strange noise. We said good morning, then he said, 'Olga, you were puzzled by my song.' I said, 'Yes, Brother Grigory, may I ask you what it was?' He replied, 'I was practising singing my Cries. All the thirty-two directions of the Compass have a Cry. I am allowed to tell you, my child, because you and your sister are spiritual young ladies who can keep secrets'. He paused for effect, then said, 'I was singing the Cry of the North.'

"He stopped again, then sang a bit more, and I said, 'Could I learn to sing like that, Brother Grigory?' He said, 'You could, my child, but you should really start young, and in any case it would take you many years; do you think you will have many more years in which to study these and other things?'

"I was a bit startled. I mean, why shouldn't I have many more years, so I stopped short and looked at him, but he just had his normal sort of inscrutably intent look, so, I asked him, 'Well, maybe my other duties would intrude?' and he said, 'Indeed, yes, they would intrude, my child, wouldn't they.' Then he finished off, 'You must go to your other duties now, mustn't you?', and he turned abruptly, you know, the way he sometimes does, and so I came away." Olga looked hard at Tatiana, hoping her wise sister might have some insight into the strange ways of Brother Grigory. Tatiana looked thoughtful.

"Cries for each of the directions? That's new to me, I must say. Why should directions need a cry? It's funny; one of his rituals of nature, I suppose."

"Shush Tatiana; he told us not to talk about that."

"Why not, when there's no one else around?"

"If Mamma or Pappa heard us talking about Brother Grigory, a monk, doing rituals related to nature, they might sack him or lock him up or something and that would be terrible."

"Oh for goodness' sake, Olly, don't be so timid, scared of your Mamma and Pappa. We're intelligent modern young women so why shouldn't we talk about everything?"

"Don't call me Olly," Olga snapped, "Or I'll call you Tatty and pull your hair and scream and tear your dress like we used to when we were young."

"Sorry, Olga, but seriously, he is a wise, learned man, so it's no wonder the majority of people don't like him, and I imagine that mostly it is because they are afraid of him. Most people can't stand someone who they feel knows more than they do."

Brother Grigory usually performed the Cries on his own, but one day a couple of weeks later Olga said,

"Tatiana, do you remember I told you the other week that I met Brother Grigory and he sang the strangest phrase to me, which he called 'The Cry of the North'?"

"Mmm, yes."

"Well, I met him again yesterday at tea-time just as he was going out. And he was singing one of his Cries again."

"Funny isn't it; you're the only one he lets hear them."

"Yes, well, he is fussy about what he says and to whom. Anyway, this time he called it, 'The Cry of the East', and do you know, it was amazing. It really sounded different from the one he called 'The Cry of the North'."

"That sounds interesting, Olga. Can you demonstrate them at all?"

"Don't know, let's see." And Olga tried to imitate the difference. The sounds were difficult to describe. The North sound was still, dimly lit, and quiet. East: full of fire, and awakens you as you listen, but also very still. South: a soft steady booming and humming sound, with long slow waves in it. West: decline, end, everything come to a halt and tensely waiting, but with stars in it. Brother Grigory did not write the Cries himself, but had inherited them from his teachers in north-eastern Siberia. He drove himself to learn all the old natural magic quickly, because he knew that his life was going to be short. He was in tune with the soul of his country and was able to foresee the disasters coming to Russia, as indeed could Olga.

Olga liked spending time with her sister. Even though she was the elder, she felt overawed by Tatiana's spirituality and leadership, and was happy to be led by her.

The imperial family's way of life was strange and unnatural anyway, with the upper-class rituals of living in ascetic conditions like the famous cold baths and narrow beds, while surrounded by the huge wealth of almost endless jewels, paintings, books, furniture, carpets, icons, altar pieces, miniatures, musical instruments, and much else, such as even floors and ceilings constructed of rare and beautiful stones. And virtuously doing their classes with their governesses and tutors. It was a fake life with no reality in it, but they accepted it because they never knew any other life and it seemed normal to them. Life always does to everybody, until something happens to wake them up. The imperial family were woken up all right, by the war in 1914 but chiefly by the revolution in 1917, but even so, by 1912 the two girls had already begun to be worried about the poor people of Russia.

Tatiana, 1912

"You know, Olga, I sometimes get really bored." Olga frowned at the interruption, then looked up. "Mmm?"

"I get really tired of things. Don't you?"

Olga was puzzled. "Well, the weather has been grey, but I'm not complaining, we needed rain…"

"Don't be such a sillyboots. You know I don't mean the weather."

"Don't say don't at me in that bossy voice. And don't call me a sillyboots. How was I to know you didn't mean the weather?"

"Oh all right, sorry, Olga. No, seriously, I do get fed up, and do you know why?"

Olga closed her book with a snap and made as if to throw it at her sister.

"Look, I'll bump you over the head with a cushion, and then you'll have something to be fed up about, with your lovely hairdo all squashed flat. Why don't you tell me what's wrong, instead of rambling on, expecting me to read your mind? I'm not Brother Grigory, you know."

"Brother Grigory doesn't read minds, and you should stop spreading rumours. He's not even here to defend himself and you shouldn't listen to servants' tales about Mamma's spiritual master."

"Look, sister dear, I was reading my book about ten minutes ago before you so rudely interrupted me. Are you, or aren't you, going to tell me why you're fed up? Speak now or forever hold your peace, because I want to go on reading, and this book is far more interesting than you wanting to complain. And for goodness' sake stop using the words 'should' and 'shouldn't' at me so much. I'm not a soldier in your own imperial private army, you know."

"It's because life is so totally predictable. I mean, Olga, look at both of us."

"I'm looking. What am I supposed to be seeing?"

"Our whole future lives are already planned to the minutest detail right up to the moment we die. Soon, Mamma will shove us off into marriages with so-called suitable males, and we'll be sold off to the highest bidders like a pair of well-bred cattle. Then it'll be the breeding stables for us both, for life, with no prospect of release or of shortening of sentence. Whereas if we were men, we'd have the option of a career in something interesting like the military, diplomacy, religion, industry, or medicine. Our prospects, as women, make me despair. Don't they you?"

"Tatiana, I appreciate what you are saying, but I do think you are working yourself up into the most awful froth, about something that we can't do anything about anyway. You have got a few more years to enjoy yourself first, and even if you end up in the breeding stables, as you so charmingly call them, well, so do all other women, and it can't be helped because it's just the way things are in this world.

"And at least for us the stables will be comfortable, not like those poor people whom we hear about from Brother Grigory. Fancy giving birth in a hovel in mid-winter, to your ninth child to add to the eight you already can't find food for, in addition to your husband injured in an accident who is dying because you can't afford a doctor. Oh, no, you and I, sister dear, are doing very nicely thank you, and have absolutely nothing to complain about." Olga opened her book and stared at it, but Tatiana was in full flow and rattled on.

"But it's the awful inevitability that gets me down more than anything. What choice have we got, none, as you've said, it's the same for all women; except of course for the few who become nuns."

Olga decided to give up trying to read, but to humour her sister instead. She shut her book and nodded. "Yes, and we can't do that even if we want to. Mamma said Pappa wouldn't allow it."

Tatiana stared. "When did she say that?"

"Oh, when I asked her a few weeks ago."

Tatiana spluttered, "You asked Mamma an important thing like that without talking to me first?"

"Tatiana dear, I don't have to clear everything I say to our parents with you first. Stop acting like a policewoman. I asked Mamma about becoming a nun, because I was interested, and I'm older than you, so it's more relevant for me, and anyway you know I'm interested in religion and that sort of thing. It happened to crop up, and you weren't there. You were out having your riding lesson but Mamma made me miss mine because I'd got a cold, and I had this great discussion with Mamma about what we two, you and I, are going to do with our lives."

"Yes, Olga, all right, but it's so crucial, so vital. I'd much rather be a sister in a monastery and work hard and pray all day and dig in a vegetable garden or write scripts down or something, than be shoved off into some unending marriage with some awful man seventy years older than me and horrible."

"Tattikins, do calm down. Don't forget, Pappa has already assured us lots of times that he won't, as you so brilliantly put it, shove us off into some awful marriage that we don't want. And in any case, if you really had the chance to get married to some awful man seventy years older than you, you'd be a fool not to take it. Look what would happen! You'd only have to put up with him for a few years, and then he's die of old age and you'd be rid of him. But you'd be in a marvellous position. You'd inherit all his money and houses and lands and things, and you could take your pick of all the lovely eligible young men who'd have been eyeing you up and down with great interest. You'd be one of the world's most desirable catches, a rich, young, beautiful widow!

"Well, that's what I'd do anyway. Ask Mamma on your own behalf about joining a monastery. Why shouldn't you, after all, as you say, it is so very important, and even if Mamma said no when I asked, well, you are good at talking to her so you might be able to wangle a different reply for yourself. And even if she still says no, you don't have to say that we two have discussed it."

"No, but she'll guess. And you know I can't bear to deceive darling Mamma. She knows we two discuss everything."

"Ye-es... but I believe she'd say we should discuss our futures. Well, I think we should. Look how isolated we are from real life. How are we supposed to know anything if we don't—"

"Olga! Stop that this minute."

"Eh? Don't you talk to me like that."

"You're criticising—"

"Shut up. I'll criticise you and Mamma and Pappa and even Brother Grigory if I want to—"

"I'll tell Mamma you're being rude—"

"Oh do get lost, Tatiana. Stand on your own feet and fight your own battles. You're too damned good for your own good, and more importantly, for mine, and you drive me up the wall. I am an intelligent young woman and perfectly entitled to speak my own mind—"

"Entitled to speak your mind? You sound like one of those dreadful socialists who are trying to destroy society."

"Yah, freedom of speech! Go on, run to Mamma and Pappa and tell them big sister wants the civil right of freedom of speech."

"You'll be out manning the barricades next."

"I might too, don't push me too far, giving me ideas. Or you'll find out one fine morning that I've hopped off to fight for the rights of the poor people."

"You and your poor people. You care more about them than you do about us!"

"Why not! I think our poor people need all the help people like me can give them. No, sister dear, I do care about 'us', but look at our family's record. Pappa has been on the throne for nearly twenty years, and if he had ruled Russia correctly, the country would by now be a paradise on Earth, with no poverty, sickness, wars, strikes, crime, or—"

"Olga! Be realistic and face facts. How can you blame all the country's woes on Pappa?"

"Quite easily. I—"

"Now, listen—"

"I can't help listening when you never stop blethering on, Tatiana. I happen to believe that the monarch has got, logically, to be ultimately responsible for all the main things which happen in his realm, and especially when he says he's an absolute ruler, like Pappa does. Don't you believe that leadership confers responsibility?"

"Well, yes, but—"

"But nothing. Pappa—"

"Shut up, Olga." Olga glared as her sister launched into one of her well-worn political diatribes. "Pappa is an unusually holy monarch, for example, unlike his ancestors and his entire court, he is actually loyal to his wife, which is almost unheard of in any emperor throughout history. He's been a good and attentive father, and he even has a resident holy man, Brother Grigory Efimovich, as an accepted advisor."

"Stop hiding behind Brother Grigory. I revere him just as much as you do. I know that Pappa is very well behaved, but Tatiana, personal morality has never been enough in a monarch. You say you're fond of history; well, read your history and you'll find that saintly kings usually fall down in some big way sooner or later. Now, I know that you'll scream at me, but I'm going to say this next bit, which I've believed for years, so listen: I would prefer Pappa had had forty mistresses and run the country better. Read the newspapers and really think about what motivates the satirists. Read those leaflets that you let the servants give you. Yes, I know about the pile of leaflets you keep tucked under your stockings in that drawer, and you do care about the poor people out there, really. If you didn't, you wouldn't chat to the servants and listen to their woes. But to continue: I do think that this country is heading for catastrophe, and I think a monarch is ultimately responsible for the state of his country."

"Catastrophe? How do you work that out?"

"Well, look what happened seven years ago."

"Oh, you mean that disturbance in St. Petersburg when some people got shot? Well, they deserved to be."

"Tatiana Nicolaeivna, they did not deserve to be."

"Yes they did. Pappa said so."

"Oh really. Pappa said so, so it's got to be true. Is that what you are saying? Tatiana, do try to think for just one minute occasionally. Why do you think a hundred thousand people came to demonstrate?"

"Pappa said they were lazy disloyal peasants who were led on by paid international agitators."

"Listen, Tatty, don't be such a twit.

"Don't call me Tatty!"

"Oh all right, sorry I called you Tatty, but honestly, you do ask for it. Those people weren't given tickets by your agitators, they all paid their own fares and expenses."

"How do you know?"

"Brother Grigory said so, and you know he knows lots of people all across the social spectrum."

"Oh he said so, did he. And what were you doing talking to him without a chaperone?"

"Stop begging the question. The fate of a hundred thousand Russian people is more important than me being chaperoned. Go on, I dare you to go and tell on me to

Mamma. I can just see it: 'Olga has been talking to Brother Grigory without a chaperone.'"

"Olga, stop being beastly about darling Mamma. She is your mother and she loves you. You're awful; you're talking about her with no respect at all."

"Listen, sister dear, I don't mind you managing the three of us girls as your own private company. Usually you're bright and dynamic. Sometimes you're even more intelligent than I am, and that's saying something, but today all you're doing is rant. Come on, get your brain together. I respect both of our parents, but I'm not talking about either of them now. I am talking about the whole Russian People. Those demonstrators were shot when they were walking along singing hymns, asking Pappa politely and respectfully for civil rights."

"Civil rights? Olga, you're a grand duchess of the ruling imperial family. Question one is, where do you pick up these dreadful socialist expressions? And question two is, how can you bring yourself to use them?"

"Tatiana, 'civil rights' is a perfectly respectable expression which the workers and people like that have been using for years—"

"Workers? Really, how could you, Olga? Where did you pick up that expression?"

"Don't interrupt me, I'm older than you, Tatiana, and I won't having you telling me what I can or cannot say. Don't be such a hypocrite. If I was using awful rude swear words you wouldn't create a fuss, but when I suggest that possibly, just possibly, Pappa and Mamma haven't been running our country the way they should, you turn purple and blow your top."

"And rightly so. I've never heard any of us say anything like what you've been saying today, so shocking, so socialist, so nonsensical…"

"And as for how I can bring myself to use socialist expressions, well, why not? I think the workers," Olga shouted the word, "the workers, deserve the support of everyone, including us. Well, I've got to go to my music lesson, and I haven't got any more time for politics at the moment, so let's resume this discussion later. And in the meantime, why don't you learn to think a bit straighter. Cheerio for now, Tatiana."

Broader Concepts

"Good day to you, my dear children." Brother Grigory greeted Olga and Tatiana at Tsarskoe Selo on a pleasant morning in 1913.

"Good day, Brother Grigory Efimovich." The girls curtseyed.

"Let us take our customary walk around the lake." They started on the usual route, keeping the lake on their right, with the girls' chaperone following at a tactful distance.

"Now today, my children, let us talk about the holy things of God." Brother Grigory paused, and the girls blessed themselves. "Today, I want to speak to you of concepts you may not have heard before.

"Now, my dear Lady Olga, after this life ends, what do you expect will happen to you?"

"Well, Brother Grigory, Mamma says that after death, God will judge me on my actions, and I'll be alive but in a different state from what I am in now. If I have been good, it will be a state of joy and happiness, and if I haven't, a place of punishment and misery where the worst punishment of all will be separation from the divine vision." Olga recited the well known words, and felt pleased with herself for remembering this important quotation from her lessons off by heart.

Brother Grigory looked her in the eye and nodded.

"Very good, my child. Now, you, Lady Tatiana, please tell me what you think shall happen after you die?"

"Oh, I hope to go straight to Heaven, a place where I'll worship and love the Lord God for ever and ever. That's what Mamma says."

Brother Grigory smiled at her confidence. "I see. Very good, my child." He paused to think, and then went on. "You both have the same idea, in other words, that Holy God rewards us after death according to what we deserve."

"Yes, Brother Grigory."

"Now, both of you, think about this. Is there a sense of time on the other side?"

There was a silence and they walked on a few yards. Then Brother Grigory decided to help the girls.

"Let us put it this way. Will you have memories? Will your lives ever change? To worship God is very fine. But if you had, for example, an unfulfilled ambition at the time you died, would you not need to fulfil it before you could be happy?"

Tatiana was busy thinking, but Olga was more straightforward.

"I've worried about that, but never dared ask in case it was forbidden or something. What do you think does happen, Brother Grigory?" Tatiana nodded in agreement.

"Well now, my children, what if I suggested that everyone has not just one life, but a series of many lives, and that in this way, such problems could be harmoniously resolved by being carried over from one life to the next until you managed to complete everything?"

Tatiana squeaked in amazement, and Olga looked taken aback. "Oh, well, er..." Brother Grigory stayed silent, and then Olga got excited.

"Goodness, Brother Grigory, that's a wonderful idea, but how can it work, I mean, it's heresy or something, isn't it?"

"Oh no, my child, not necessarily. It's a very old belief in some parts of the world. It's called Reincarnation, and many of the world's great religions believe in it."

"Oh, that's interesting." She frowned, seeing all sorts of ramifications and trying to work through them. "But, Brother Grigory, how can we not have it in our belief, if so many other religions have got it? I mean, something either does exist or doesn't exist. What do you think?"

"Better for your learning and instruction, if I ask, what do you think? Now, my child, let us have your views please."

Tatiana glowered because she had as usual been ready to dive in with instant wisdom. But out of good manners towards Brother Grigory she kept quiet and let Olga speak first.

"Heavens. Well, I think it's a terribly exciting idea, Brother Grigory. Far more interesting than having only one life. I'd have lots of chances to do different things, like, for example, I'd love to be a man and have a really great life being a soldier or a diplomat or something, instead of just being shoved off into some awful marriage like we women all are. It is such a brand new idea that I'm just a bit worried that it may be heresy, but if you suggested it, Brother Grigory, it can't be actually wrong in the moral sense. I know, I'll do some research. Pappa or our tutors might have books that mention it." She stopped, to give Tatiana a turn.

"And you, Lady Tatiana. Let us have your views on this now please."

Tatiana took a deep breath. "Brother Grigory, this is the one of the most exciting days of my life because you've answered one of my biggest questions. Like my sister, I'd wondered, but never dared ask, about that problem of dying with unfulfilled ambitions. Yet it explains so many things, doesn't it?"

Brother Grigory smiled and nodded. "It does, my children."

Tatiana went on. "And how strange we wondered about the same thing for years and never mentioned it to each other."

"Yes, indeed."

"Yes, it is funny," agreed Olga. "We normally discuss everything." She paused. "But, Brother Grigory, what actually happens? How often do we have a life, and do we always meet the same people, and live in the same country, or what?"

"The idea, my child, is to gain wide experience, and progress towards mental, physical and spiritual perfection. Nobody knows all the details, but some people believe that we have lives in many different places and conditions. Others say that if we have been wicked we may go so far back as to be reborn as animals..."

"Ooh, awful."

"...and if we have been extra good we may be allowed many years on the other side, enjoying the Gift of the Divine Vision before coming down into rebirth again."

"Oh I see, Brother Grigory," said Tatiana, "We have heaven or hell like the church says, but only for a while, and then we have another life."

"Or, you could say, my child, that we bring our heaven or hell back with us to this earthly plane, according to what we deserve to have next time."

Both girls looked impressed.

"So, let us go on to your questions, Olga. How often we have a life, depends on how we have behaved. And your other point, about people: the answer to this is that we meet different people from life to life, to broaden our experience."

"My goodness, Brother Grigory," said Tatiana, "thank you for telling us all this, it is so very important and interesting; but why haven't we done it in our lessons?"

"My children, learned men love to disagree over something important, and in that way, create more topics to discuss, so that they may sit perpetually over cups of tea or glasses of their favourite wines, talking and feeling important, but actually accomplishing nothing, and wasting their whole lives."

Olga giggled.

Tatiana was shocked. "But then they are misleading the people."

"Men love to argue over reincarnation. You see, even though it is logical, you will understand that it cannot ever be proved. So as it cannot be proved, my child, you cannot absolutely claim that they are misleading anyone."

"Well..." Tatiana was uncertain, and, unusually, she faded into silence for a moment or two.

"Olga, my child, you were commenting on how a thing must either exist or not exist, and so, why do we not teach reincarnation when other great world religions do? I commend you for having the insight to ask this intelligent question, and my answer is that it's not that we don't teach reincarnation, but down the years, it has become pushed to the back, behind other facets of our belief system. Now, some prelates say that it should be taught regardless because it is true. But an influential majority say the people should be taught to focus on the life they are in, because this is enough to keep them busy, and also, if people think that the life they are in is their only chance of salvation they will work harder than they would if they knew they have further opportunities in the future."

"I see, Brother Grigory," said Olga. "It's understandable, but I think it's unfair, making all those people stay ignorant, not knowing what's going to happen to them."

"Yes," agreed Tatiana. "It's not right to teach untruth, or half or three quarters of the whole truth. Who do those prelates think they are? They may have high rank, but that is only because they're rich enough to have had schooling, and for all they know, some of their people may be very holy even though they are poor. To be holy and poor is not unheard of. We are told The Lord Jesus Himself was one of these."

"True, my child, Blessed be His Holy Name, but I regret you will find in life that some people prefer political advantage or career advancement to truth."

Tatiana smiled sadly and nodded. "Yes, Brother Grigory. I've already found that happens, even in this great country of ours."

Brother Grigory nodded to Tatiana with great respect, then stayed quiet for a bit to let the girls think. The party carried on until they got to a place where they often halted on their walks, a shallow, muddy bit of lake with a bridge over a narrow place, where mature deciduous trees crowded the bank, like giants holding a conference, Olga used to think as a little girl. Still deep in their thoughts, they turned back.

Brother Grigory changed the mood. "Well, my children, I have enjoyed our meeting, and I trust that you good ladies have found it instructive."

The girls nodded and smiled, "Oh yes, Brother Grigory, thank you very much!" and Olga went on, "We'll have a lovely time now, arguing with our tutors about religion and history in class. I bet they'll be surprised what we have learnt from you, Brother Grigory."

"Oh, my child, please do not do that yet."

"But if we know something, can't we talk about it?"

"I would prefer you to keep it among yourselves and within your family circle, my child, because it is better not to talk too freely of controversial religious matters with too large a number of people. Please think it over for a few months first, and then you will know how much to say and to whom."

"Oh, very well, Brother Grigory, I see."

"We must discuss again these matters of religion and philosophy. But now, let us return indoors and find ourselves some tea."

The Girls' Future

Count Worthton was worried about the two elder girls, because he felt that time was passing quickly and they were still treated as children, so he decided to prod their parents into thinking more deeply about their futures.

The audience took place in a private drawing room in the palace at Tsarskoe Selo. It was a relatively small square-shaped room, with taupe walls and a wood block floor, white plasterwork on ceiling and walls, and wide windows with apricot coloured velvet curtains. On the wall opposite the windows was an enormous gold-framed mirror, and the furniture was early nineteenth century. The windows looked out on to views of exquisitely manicured lawns and flowers.

Nicholas sat in an upholstered upright chair, and Alexandra perched near him on the end of a sofa. The count took a chair opposite Nicholas from where he could see Alexandra's face from the side. After the formal bows, introductions and compliments, Count Worthton got down to business.

"The Grand Duchesses Olga and Tatiana will no doubt be married in due course to eminent and suitable gentlemen."

Nicholas looked at Alexandra for guidance. She glowered at him and frowned at the count, resenting his intervention in what she considered a family matter, but too cautious of her reputation to tell him bluntly to go away and mind his own business.

Eventually Nicholas took the lead and said, "Indeed, yes, my dear Count."

"I have taken the liberty of giving some thought to the futures of these two ladies. Might I put to you, sir and to you, madam, my conclusions?"

Nicholas frowned, then nodded, and Alexandra continued to look frosty.

"First, let us consider the Grand Duchess Olga. This is a young lady of considerable intelligence, with abilities in languages, music and religion. I feel that she would be well utilised if married into an eminent family in a country located near to Russia. The selection of her husband requires careful thought to ensure that her talents are used and she is happy.

"No doubt your majesties have already given thought to the future of this young lady. I appreciate the opportunity to offer a humble contribution."

The count looked firmly at Nicholas and Alexandra. He was aware of his own spiritual authority and knew that now was a time when he could justifiably pull rank to persuade them into action. Sensing his moral superiority, the imperial couple sat still, resenting his attempt to teach them but afraid to contradict him. He continued.

"From my observations I believe that Olga would be unhappy if sent far from Russia because she is such an intensely patriotic young lady, too much so, I feel, although it is too late now to alter this. She has worked hard and consistently at her lessons, and she has also been self-disciplined enough to do extra private study in the subjects which she enjoys, notably religion and music. It is a pity that the religious life is not open to her."

Meanwhile, Nicholas and Alexandra were glancing at each other and squirming furiously, amazed at the count's knowledge of Olga's character. The count could feel their bewildered thoughts, "How did this upstart self-appointed advisor find out all this about a member of our family, when he spends so much time abroad, and how much does he talk about us to other people?" Alexandra looked daggers at Nicholas, willing him to comment, and with luck, shut the count up. Nicholas said,

"My wife and I are notably impressed at your familiarity with the Grand Duchess Olga's character and abilities."

The count bowed acknowledgement.

"Your grace is kind." He paused politely to show appreciation of the compliment. "To continue. I understand Olga enjoys her military duties, and this is a good point which I feel could be built on. Because she is a female the profession of arms is unfortunately closed to her, but her care for the men in the regiments of which she is titular officer in charge can be broadened into care and concern for all her people, the men and women in her wider world of adulthood. Further, she must learn that feeling care is not enough, but that care has to be shown, mainly in physical manifestation, or in the eyes of those cared about it cannot and does not exist."

The count paused to give Nicholas and Alexandra time to realise he was trying to teach them too, but alas his words did not impinge. He pulled a faint wry face and went on.

"Olga's chief virtues are patriotism, devotion and truthfulness. She also has humanitarian potential, and I see her perhaps visiting poor houses in slum areas and giving food, clothing, friendship and medical help. This would show the people that their new princess has taken them to her heart, and they would think well of Russia.

"A woman in high position can do great good, and she should be taught to appreciate her material wealth and share it with her people. As indeed has been the case with the Grand Duchess Olga. A well brought up young person, who will serve her people well, whoever they are."

The count paused politely to show his emperor and empress that he knew his place, as a guest in their court and therefore required to follow their standard procedures of manners and culture. When he realised that they had nothing to say at that point, he went on.

"Next, allow me, if I may, to venture some carefully studied observations about the Grand Duchess Tatiana. Now, this young lady is a very different person from the Grand Duchess Olga. Her talents are of the spirit. She is a masterful young woman with great potential for leadership, and she requires careful handling. Her husband must be selected with extreme care. She must herself have a large say in the matter, but based on facts, not hearsay.

"More even than Grand Duchess Olga, the Lady Tatiana needs to circulate in society, not simply to meet a husband, but also to gain skill in handling people. All the grand duchesses will need this. At present, everyone they meet is courteous to them because of who they are, but later in life they will undoubtedly meet people who are not graciously disposed towards them and will, rather, insult and attack them because of who they are."

Nicholas and Alexandra looked sceptical at this last, but the count knew that he must emphasise it.

"There will be people who will oppose them because of who they are, particularly in company. The grand duchesses must learn to handle a wide cross-section of people, not solely here in Russia, but elsewhere too.

"To return to the Grand Duchess Tatiana. Because her gifts are chiefly in the realm of the spirit, she must be married to a husband who will treat her as an intellectual equal. Such a man may prove difficult to find, but it is essential, otherwise she will be totally wasted and unhappy with perhaps even her life cut short.

"Even though she is quicker at music than Olga, it will be less important to her.

"Do not allow minor details to sway your judgement of who is suitable for your daughters, but rather see the broad view and consider in each case, the young lady's overall character.

"Tatiana might do well in a country some distance from Russia; for example, there are several eligible German princes whom I am sure you have already considered. I suggest that she starts learning German if she has not already done so. In any case, Germany is an important neighbour, and one which I hope will be friendly to Russia far into the future."

He stopped, and the little group sat silent, Alexandra still rigid with suspicion and disapproval, and Nicholas high on the potion Brother Grigory was trying to wean him off. The count knew them both only too well, and, aware that he had not got endless time to kick them into shape, he decided it was time to be blunt.

"Your majesties have kindly heard me and given me your time. However, may I point out that the young ladies are both old enough to be betrothed, if not yet married, and I respectfully submit to your majesties that it is time action was taken to ensure a fulfilled and happy future for both of them. Thank you for your patience and attention."

The count made his regulation bows, and left.

Nicholas shook his head and looked at Alexandra.

"Well, dear, all that was most interesting, and our excellent Count Worthton has certainly found out more about our family than I would have imagined he easily could do, considering the amounts of time he spends abroad. But he did seem to be bringing up some good points, don't you think?"

"No, Nicky dear, I don't agree with you. I think he is being premature, and furthermore, I do wish that he would not come in here and tell us how to run our family as well as regularly telling us how to run our empire. He really is out of order, and thinks far too much of himself.

"In any case, the girls aren't grown up yet, so I think we should leave it all a bit longer."

River Magic

Brother Grigory knew that Olga must learn about the Devic Kingdom, the invisible beings, great and small, who manipulate the energies of plant life, air, earth, water and fire. These living creatures range from tiny flower fairies, to lordly beings who are like great living clouds of dynamic energy, and govern vast currents of air and tide in accordance with divine law without fear or favour. He knew that Olga would use the knowledge in her near future, by which he meant a life or two. She was a good pupil, absorbing all he said and voluntarily doing her own extra research. In devic studies she outshone Tatiana. Brother Grigory found that Tatiana had barriers caused by her righteous and correct attitude, but Olga was mentally free, and forged ahead. Tatiana did not need the knowledge, but he had to let her be present for these classes. It did no harm, she might benefit, and he could not risk his tuition of the girls being stopped by gossip which would start if he spoke to one of the girls alone even with a chaperone present. Many courtiers were hostile and jealous, and he was not going to hand ammunition to them on a plate.

He was well aware of the spiritual law that forbade him to tell the girls bluntly about their former lives, but he could narrate stories which he knew were about them, provided he implied that the stories were about other people. One experience sequence which he wanted to bring back into Olga's conscious mind was an important and quite recent life, about eight hundred years before, when she was the chief high priestess in a society which still did a lot of energy work in cooperation with the Devic Kingdom. He narrated the story one day when he accompanied the two elder girls on one of their regular walks. Instead of conducting them on the usual route round the lake, he found a convenient seat for them all at the bottom of the sloping lawn. The girls' chaperone found a place twenty yards away, and tactfully sat knitting. Brother Grigory sat silent for a couple of minutes, aware of how important this afternoon's tuition would be in Olga's future lives, and praying for inspiration to enable him to teach her aright. Then he took a deep breath and began his tale.

"Once upon a time there was a girl who lived in a big tribe on the west side of the River Lena, that mighty stream of eastern Siberia. Her Pappa was one of the chiefs. She was educated from babyhood to be the head of the wise women, and was taught all their female magic.

"She was chosen at birth and trained from birth. When she was little, discipline was strict and she was subject to what seemed to her then to be an endless list of niggling constrictions. Sometimes she got upset and rebelled, but this was a necessary stage, and indeed, her teachers told her later that her periodic fits of naughtiness and disobedience were good because they were a sign of initiative. Initiative in its place was looked for in trainee ritualists, because rather than being fixed rigidly, their tribal lore was considered by them to be open to change when good new ideas were introduced. As Chief Woman Ritualist she would be expected, no, she would absolutely have to be able to make the right decision about proposed changes.

"When she was four years old, she was forbidden for several months to walk on the ground. This was to let the hereditary tribal spirit take up his dwelling in her in the way that he required. She was female and the ground was female but this particular tribal spirit was male, so he would find it difficult to ground his polarity in her, and needed time. If she had touched the ground, the spirit's energy would have gone out through her feet into the greater female, the ground, and the whole process of grounding the spirit in her would have had to be started all over again. It was quite an awkward phase. She had to be carried about by people, and found it very difficult. She sulked and threw things and tore her clothes and cried, saying she wanted to be like all the other little girls and go out and play. Sometimes the adults around her were sympathetic but other times they thumped her to persuade her to obey. So she had to put up with the boredom and frustration of this phase.

"Later, when about fourteen, she asked why the grounding had had to be done when she was so young. She said she could have done it more easily now, because she was older and had more understanding, and would find the discipline less hard. But the answer was that the grounding had to be done at that age so as to be completed before she could start other parts of her priestly training.

"She had to attend court meetings from the age of four, to prepare for the political part of her job. Oh dear. No doubt it was terribly good for her. At first she was standing all the time, as a junior and very young trainee, for hours and hours, and she got tired, stiff and thirsty. She had to wear ceremonial dresses of woven gold thread, and the threads scratched and tickled until she got to screaming point. If she fidgeted, one of her Pappa's courtiers would thump her with his staff of office and growl terrible threats, like extra duties, or no water, or no supper, which was a clever one as she liked her food. She stood there, a puzzled little girl among all those grown-ups who looked enormously tall in their ceremonial robes and big headdresses, and talked in big long words that she couldn't understand. Occasionally her Pappa would let her sit on his knee for a rest, or her Auntie, another senior member of the court, would pass her a tasty treat which she would munch hungrily. This way she learned that it was good to temper strictness with mercy, and sternness with humour. Later she began to understand what she was hearing. Older members asked her about the discussions, and she enjoyed showing off her own ideas. By the time she was fifteen she was allowed to sit down, showing that she was now a full member of the court.

"One of her main tasks was to work with one of the principle local deities, the Master Deva in charge of her section of the River Lena; you might call him the local River God. When she was grown up and was the fully initiated and trained Chief Woman Ritualist she did this many times. In fact, she had the power to summon him to her presence. The only other person who could do this was the Chief Man Ritualist. The woman who taught her to do the summoning lost the power to do it when she formally, and by ancient secret ritual, conferred her powers upon this girl, so that only one woman and one man could at any time carry out the summoning.

"When the River Deva appeared to her, she actually saw him come up out of the water. First she would do her secret chants, dances, fasts, dieting and other preparations. She did the first part of the ritual in her own dwelling on the outskirts of their town. Then she went down to the bank of the River and for the last two hours worked there. This stage consisted mainly of chanting. There were also magical hand, foot and body movements, especially at the very climax of the working when she also made a sudden shout and clapped her hands loudly at a particular angle.

"Then she stood rigidly, breathing carefully. She and her two magical apprentice assistants waited, mentally and physically keyed up and in a high state of mystical awareness and tension.

"The River Deva would rise from under the surface of the River and go up straight, to about thirty or forty feet in the air. At this stage he appeared as a twenty foot long, oval cloud of energy, mainly silvery-grey and shot through with gold sparks. Slowly he would make his body coalesce, dimming the light, until he looked the shape of a man, thirty feet above the River, facing upstream.

"After a brief pause, he turned slowly and faced her. She made more movements, summoning him, and he slowly floated nearer, descending, until he stood eleven and a half feet from her and a foot above the water, facing her. Now, his appearance was that of a man of her tribe, dressed in ceremonial robes. I will describe these in detail as this is important.

"The overall colour was pure crimson. His magnificent full-length cloak was crimson, and looked like thick fine wool. Under this he wore many other garments. Again, the predominant colour was crimson, but there was some greyish blue and some silvery grey, and a few streaks of very dark grey, perhaps black. As part of his act at appearing as a human being, he wore a belt. This looked like fine, thick leather, beautifully treated, and covered with gold.

"He appeared to have hair, thick, black, long wonderful hair, that was curled and stood out all round his head like a halo. He wore shoes of soft leather that clung to the shape of the foot. Like the shoes on illustrations of fairies, they had toes that curled over, and the piece at the back of the ankle was elongated and fell downwards behind the foot.

"He had the face of a man of her tribe. His face was beautiful and magnificent, and his expression was solemn and unearthly. She felt joy and exultation when she gazed at him. He looked mature but not old. His face showed wisdom, breadth of vision, and beauty of soul. He looked like a mature man of her tribe, but like a man above other men, with abilities beyond those of ordinary men.

"He would stop above the water. He hovered over the water and never came over the land. There was always a pause while they gazed at each other, the human woman and the non-human man. They examined each other through the aperture which their mutual magic had created in the curtain that normally separates their kingdoms.

"Communication was carried out in the secret, sacred language which her magical master, the previous Chief

Woman Ritualist, had taught her. She spoke out loud to the River Deva, and he formed his replies so that they sounded to her ears like speech. His voice was light tenor, with a pervasive single musical tone through it. It was definitely not a normal male voice, but neither did it sound at all like a female human's voice. It was simply different, a mark of the otherness of the speaker.

"It is interesting to note that up to that time, within the past thousand years, her group of people still carried in their culture the knowledge of an actual physical language that gave communication with a member of the Devic Kingdom. Secret languages are mentioned in many traditions; I have met mentions of them in the parts which I have visited of the Russian Empire, the Holy Land, and Europe, and it occurs to me that some of these languages may be used for devic communication. I have seen mentions of 'the language of the birds' and 'the green language'. These may be codenames, but would probably also refer to the function and purpose of the language. The French saint, Jeanne d'Arc, is said to have used a secret language to communicate with her saints, Saint Michael the Archangel, Saint Catherine and Saint Margaret. Magic chants are found throughout the world, and sometimes even crop up in children's fairy tales, and my master in Siberia told me, too, that birds are devic messengers.

"It is worth noting that before she could use her tribe's own secret language to converse with the Lena River Deva, she first of all had to be capable of bringing him into her presence, and also, to conduct the communication in the right ritual manner. This is an important proviso that applied to her own particular case, but it probably applies to all communications carried out formally across the divide between the human and devic kingdoms.

"By the time the River Deva had arrived in front of her, she was in a deep mystical trance state and was oblivious to everything around her. She could see only the Deva, and dimly in the background, his dwelling, the River, and nearby river vegetation. Her two magical apprentice assistants sat silently several yards away, not moving or speaking throughout the three and a half hours of the manipulation.

"Note also that when she spoke to the Deva, her assistants could not hear her voice in such a way that they could have picked out words; all they heard was a rushing, harmonious, rising and falling humming sound, similar to the sound of a river. It was of course strictly prohibited for them to try and imitate the sound; for this the penalty was death either sooner or later, usually sooner. This is not because the priestess or the Deva killed them, not at all, but because they would have infringed a law which has existed from time immemorial and comes from a very high realm. The assistants never saw the River Deva. All they were allowed to know, was that the Chief Woman Ritualist was praying to the Gods for the good of their tribe.

"The meeting would start with ritual greetings. Then the priestess and the River Deva would discuss recent events. They would move on from there to general subjects relating to the long-term wellbeing of the tribe. After the greetings, the conversation proceeded similar to normal talk between two adult human beings.

"When they both felt that all subjects had been covered, they carried out the parting ritual. They thanked each other, and paid compliments to each other's devotion to the wellbeing of the tribe. Then the priestess did the closing ritual. The opening in the web between the realms had to be closed, and the River Deva had to be helped to return to his normal state and to his place above the River. He would then himself decide whether to hover above the River for a time or to descend straight away into the water which was his customary dwelling.

"The priestess brought herself down from her high mystical trance state. Without speaking, she returned to her dwelling. There she would ritually bath in special herbs and spices, and change her clothes; sometimes, according to which ritual was performed at the River, she was required to burn, secretly, all the clothing and equipment used. She did a long session of prayers of thanks to the Gods. These were the more general gods of Earth, Water, Fire, Sky, Trees, and so on, rather than their particular tribal God, the Deva who dwelt in the River and with whom she had just been communicating. This part of the ritual was very important. Their religion insisted that heartfelt thanks must be given for all favours received from Heaven, and that if this was not done, favours already received might be taken away, and future favours withheld.

"These specialised River Deva Rituals were carried out on a regular basis, and she could also carry one out if the need arose, for example, if hardship or military attack looked like threatening the tribe. Sometimes she would carry one out if she felt it necessary, and at other times a solemn convocation of the Tribal Seniors, of whom she was one of the most important, was called, and the Chief Woman Ritualist and the Chief Man Ritualist would agree, in very guarded and ritually formal language, to 'pray to the Gods of the Tribe', this being the code for the High Magic they practised in their own secret rituals.

"Of course she had many other duties; baptising new babies in the Water of the River was one of her favourite tasks. She loved welcoming these new, yet old, little souls into the bosom of the tribe. She also blessed crops and led worship, and spent quite some time at certain seasons of the year deciding, during fasting, prayer and contemplation, exactly when and where the first seeds of the new crops should be planted.

"This priestess led a very happy and fulfilled life, and passed on at over eighty years of age after happily and gracefully conferring her Magical Powers upon her priestly successor."

Brother Grigory stared Olga in the eye. She looked stunned. Memories, scenes, colours, trees, were swirling round in her head. She stared into Brother Grigory's eyes, into those ancient, deep eyes, wise beyond belief, full of teaching and guiding. Then his eyes and his expression were normal again. She looked round her. The lawns and the lake were the same, but she felt different: uplifted, and a bit puzzled. Devas. Rivers. And into her mind came a vision of a stone figure with a face carved on it. The five foot tall, conical stone had rested deep in the River Lena for millennia, and yet it was eternally her stone. One day she would find it, but not yet. How she longed to see that stone again. Again? Now, why did that word occur to her? Life was full of wonders and mysteries.

"Life, my dear ladies, is full of wonders and mysteries," Brother Grigory said. Olga nodded, wide-eyed. She wanted to sit and think. They all sat quietly for ten minutes. Then, without speaking, they decided to go back indoors and find tea.

Interview, 1913

Soon after the discussion about the two elder girls' futures, Count Worthton approached Nicholas and Alexandra again. This time, he persuaded them to allow him to interview the girls and pass on to them some of his wide knowledge of diplomacy and his international point of view. The meeting took place at Tsarskoe Selo. The four sat formally, and the girls' chaperone sat at the far end of the room, working at a piece of embroidery on the small hand-held frame she favoured. Count Worthton opened the conversation.

"Their imperial majesties have graciously consented to allow your imperial highnesses to meet Reverend Brother Grigory Efimovich Rasputin-Novykh and myself today, as part of your education, to discuss foreign affairs and your future part in them."

Olga, as elder, spoke first.

"Monsieur le Comte, Grand Duchess Tatiana Nicolaeivna and myself are honoured. We understand that you have been working in international diplomacy for many years, and we appreciate the opportunity to learn from you on this your rare and valued visit to our country."

"The pleasure is all on my side, madam."

Everybody sat looking gracious for a minute or two, the girls waiting for one of the adults to start the discussions, then Count Worthton continued.

"First, I will ask about your interests, and the concerns which you have about your country."

He had been warned, although he already knew, that even though Tatiana was taller she was not the elder. He spoke to Olga.

"If I might begin with you, madam."

"Thank you, monsieur." Olga thought about what she had prepared. She took a deep breath and started.

"My concerns about my country are varied and intense. May I speak frankly in your company, monsieur?"

The count raised an eyebrow slightly, although he already knew how deep-thinking Olga was.

"Yes, madam. Our discussions will not go further than this room." He glanced firmly at Tatiana, who gave him a polite glare. Olga went on.

"Monsieur le Comte, this country is heading for ruin, and I can prove this by bringing up instances from our history. I totally condemn all my ancestors for their actions, for their mania in always conquering new lands and then not showing any interest in the peoples they have conquered. We are too ready to plunge our men, whom I love and value, into terrible wars, and then, when they are broken and disabled, what do we do to help them, or to help them to help themselves, we do absolutely nothing, nothing, monsieur, and when we do not want them to come and fight our maniacally egotistical wars for us we ignore them.

"Monsieur, it is not right, and I think that we as a ruling family are a disgrace. I think we should provide love, light, leadership and help, but when we go out we are surrounded by soldiers, and are cut off from the people whom we so ostentatiously call 'ours', as though we were afraid of them. They need us, and here we are in nineteen-thirteen, three hundred years since our ancestor Michael took over, and what have we got to show for it? Millions of our people live in terrible poverty..." Her throat began to hurt and she ground to a halt, looking distressed, then rallied.

"For example, monsieur, I will soon come in to a fortune, and I wish to use most of it on charitable projects, to help those poor ill babies in the terrible hovels and the starving children. But Her Imperial Majesty forbids me. She says I can give a little bit of relief here and there but have to keep most of it as a dowry. A dowry! She says Russia will be shamed if I do not have an enormous dowry, but I think, on the other hand, that Russia would be a greater country and less shamed if within our borders we had no poverty, no poor little crying babies who look with trusting eyes to their fathers and mothers who grieve themselves almost to death because they are unable to provide food, than that a grand duchess goes into marriage with a huge dowry. I argued a little, but Mamma got ever so angry so I stopped.

"Besides, I have vowed that I will never leave my country to live elsewhere, that is to say, I only would if I thought that I could help it better by leaving. When I marry, I want it to be to a good Russian man who loves Russia the way I do and wants to live here to show how much he cares for this country, and not go swanning about to international pleasure resorts which are useless haunts of sin and waste."

She ran out of steam, while Count Worthton looked at her with great respect. This was the only meeting he would have with the girls for a long time and he wanted to teach them as much as he could.

"Madam, do you have views on how you might help your country more?"

"Oh, monsieur, I rack my brains continually. If I were a man I could choose a career. But it's dreadful being a woman. I sometimes feel that I am just a beautiful pawn, to be utilised by contracting a marriage for His Imperial Majesty's political gain. I do feel this in myself, even though His Imperial Majesty has graciously assured us girls that he would never exert pressure on us to go into a marriage for his political advantage. Despite this, I still fear marriage, because due to my strenuous conscience I worry that I might voluntarily contract an unhappy marriage if I saw it as being for the good of the country as a whole. I don't even want to marry. I'd far rather join a convent because then I could work and pray all day, dig vegetables or write old scripts or similar work, and that would be far more useful than being a pretty cypher.

"Of course if I were a man, I could look forward to being emperor, but when my ancestor changed the rules to forbid women to succeed to the throne he did such damage to Russia because he deprived it of my potential rulership and I know that I could have done the job well. That rule is so unfair and wicked, monsieur, and I have been angry about it ever since I was about ten, when I first read about it and realised what it was depriving me of. Once at luncheon I raised the matter with my, with Their Imperial Majesties, but they got so angry that time that I felt it wasn't worth while to ask them again, and anyway I never got brave enough to do so."

Tatiana was looking stunned; she thought Olga was quite out of order. Olga tried bravely to recover. She realised that Count Worthton could see she was deeply depressed and frustrated. Olga was looking straight at him and the kindly light from his eyes cheered her up a little.

"I cannot offer you much comfort, madam, but I may be able to point out a few suggestions regarding your future life pattern. First, do you speak many languages?"

"Oh, yes, monsieur, we all speak French and English as well as Russian, and I like German too."

"This is valuable because it gives you access to those people and their cultures."

Olga had always found it difficult to conceal her feelings, and now she sounded disgruntled.

"Oh yes, monsieur, that would be the case if we two girls ever got out."

"Madam, I do not follow."

"We hardly ever meet anybody, we are closeted in our palaces because our brother is ill and we are told that we have to stay away from the people in order to protect him from sickness influences. But how can we show the people that we care unless we meet them? It's been the same all our lives, and now it is nearly too late because we are almost adults and I can only look forward to wasting time here doing more studies and classes until I get married. But after I am married, I will definitely look for ways to use my wealth in helping people. I'm going to disguise myself and walk round the streets and the villages giving money and clothes as presents to poor people."

"You really want to help your people, madam?"

"Yes, monsieur."

"I feel that Her Imperial Majesty may have a point though."

"But it cannot be right that I have so much wealth, if I use it as a dowry while children starve in hovels."

"You might help your people better by setting up hospitals and schools, than by going out and giving coins to people you meet in the streets."

Olga dug her toes in. "I want to help the poorest; not those who can afford schooling and doctors, but those who can't. There are people dying and desperate, monsieur; it's terrible. Why can't I walk round St. Petersburg with a bag of coins and hand help to mothers with little starving girls and boys? I'd rather do that first; then, when no one is actually lying in the streets dying from hunger, I can start hospitals, schools, and libraries, to help teach them how not to get poor and ill again."

"Madam, I disagree with you, because a piecemeal approach is not ideal in the long run."

He paused, and Olga struggled to look polite. Count Worthton was mollified, and continued.

"Suppose, madam, that you have two million roubles."

Olga looked interested; she liked facts and figures, so long as she didn't have to do all the work.

"Now, either you could spend an awful lot of time and energy finding two hundred thousand of the poorest people and handing them ten roubles each. This would give them relief, but once only, for a short time."

"But at least it would save some lives, monsieur." Olga was almost jumping up and down with frustration and fury.

Count Worthton gave her a reproachful look, but decided to ignore the interruption to his flow of thought. "Or you could invest your valuable time and wealth in projects which would help to cure the people of the inherited stupidity and ignorance which cause the poverty you deplore."

Olga refused to give up. "You mean hospitals, schools, and so on, monsieur? But this would mean yet more things for those who can already afford such benefits. I want to help those who have nothing."

"But you could do, madam, by setting up foundations in poor areas."

"Oh yes, I suppose so." She paused. "It would use time more efficiently. And I could show the people that I cared, by going out among them to visit the foundations, inspecting the work and hurrying it up, and thanking the workmen." She stopped arguing, and did some thinking.

"May I ask, madam: if you are as cut off from the people as you say you are, how do you know that this poverty of which you speak so eloquently, really exists?" Count Worthton was determined to give Olga a hard time and to push some sense into her head in an attempt to make her base her actions on logic rather than the emotional reactions by which she tended to be ruled.

Olga wondered whether to tell Count Worthton that it was Brother Grigory who talked to her and Tatiana about such interesting subjects, which she enjoyed a lot more than some of the stuff they did in class.

"I keep my eyes open during our journeys and sometimes catch sight of terribly destitute people. I hear babies crying; babies don't cry when they are content, but only when they are hungry or cold or neglected, and there are far too many unhappy babies in Russia."

She looked enquiringly at Brother Grigory and he nodded so she went on.

"Also, our Brother in God, Brother Grigory Efimovich, sometimes spends his valued time talking to us, telling us of

91

his travels round our vast dominions. He has seen the horrifying squalor to which many of our people have been reduced; reduced, in my opinion, by the policies pursued by our family down the centuries. After all, it is said that by their fruits you shall know them. Oh, I know some people are all right, but they are only a minority."

Olga stopped. She could feel Tatiana disapproving, but ignored her, and looked politely but firmly at the two men. Count Worthton gazed at Olga with great respect, regretting the waste of her potential.

"Madam, I sympathise with your frustration, but although unfortunately I am unable to assist you in concrete terms I find it heartening that you are so determined to find out how your people live."

"I thank you, monsieur," said Olga miserably. "But as you know, because I am a woman I am unable to help my people much at the moment. Though in a few years' time when I get married," she pulled a face, "I will be freer to look into your idea of setting up charitable foundations. But occasionally I AM going to go out with a big bag of coins and make gifts to destitute people." She took a deep breath. "Monsieur, I thank you sincerely for spending time instructing me in my duties. You have given me some new ideas, and I will definitely use them in my future life."

"It is my pleasure, madam."

There was a pause. Olga used to sitting still, so she simply relaxed. Everyone realised that Count Worthton would now interview Tatiana.

"Madam," Tatiana gave Count Worthton her authoritative look but it did not bother him; he looked right back at her and she retreated a bit mentally. "May I ask your ambitions and interests?"

"Monsieur, I also appreciate your valued expertise and time. I too regret the waste of our talents just because we are women, but I do, however, realise that there are paths I can follow within the limitations inflicted upon us. It is less immediately vital for me than it is for Grand Duchess Olga Nicolaeivna, because I am a year-and-a-half younger than she is. At present I am in the last stages of my education, and after that I will be occupied by court duties until I am married."

The count wanted to draw her out. "What are your best subjects, madam?"

"I am good at music and languages, and I enjoy writing, monsieur."

"Which languages are you studying?"

"French and English, monsieur. Also I have to learn German, but I find it difficult."

Olga felt smug. She was better than Tatiana at German.

"I see, madam. And I understand you already have court duties."

"Yes, monsieur, but not many yet." She paused. Count Worthton stayed silent, so she went on. "People speculate endlessly and with great and intrusive curiosity about whom my sister and I will marry, but I do not yet concern myself with marriage. At present I am working at the skills I shall need, namely social and court skills, management, and languages, because later on I shall be busy with duties. My sister and I are very different. People think we're the same because we are close in age and look alike. And they think I am the elder because I am taller, which is annoying to my sister. But I mention all these details, monsieur, because we are so isolated from the ordinary people. Within our family we hold long discussions about the state of our country. Our tutors and governesses are excellent, and help us immensely. Brother Grigory Efimovich assists us with various in-depth studies on theology, philosophy, and nature. He also informs us about the Russian People, from whom we do feel somewhat cut off."

Tatiana looked at Brother Grigory. He had been giving centre stage to Count Worthton, but felt that this was a good time to join in.

"My Brother Count, it has been my honour and interest over the years to converse with the Grand Duchesses Olga and Tatiana. I've observed how bored and isolated they are, and deplore the waste of their brainpower."

Olga sighed and nodded; Tatiana looked wistful.

"I can only hope that the good ladies are married to partners who respect their intellects. Things will not improve for them until they leave the court, but I think they will find it a relief to move out. The waste of Grand Duchess Olga's talents is a great crime. She would have made an excellent Empress of All the Russias." Olga politely tried not to glower.

"The young ladies don't know, but several years ago, I did raise with His Imperial Majesty the question of the succession. We were having a chat together, just the two of us, man to man, and Her Imperial Majesty was not present. I suggested that, in view of Tsarevich Alexis' illness, His Majesty change the rules to allow Olga to come to the throne should Alexis die in childhood. His Majesty was most displeased. At first he laughed, more than I have ever seen him laugh. 'My pretty little Olga, inheriting my throne?' he said when he recovered. He had thought I was joking. I assured him that I was, on the contrary, most serious, and reminded him that Russia has in her past had excellent empresses. He suddenly became irate and accused me of trying to tell him how to run his empire.

"I soothed his feelings and he repeated his usual refrain, that he was an autocrat, and therefore, which is the word he uses, therefore, he cannot change anything that he has received from his forebears. I felt it not exactly the time to remind him that in nature, only things that accept change have got any chance of surviving over long periods of time. By mutual unspoken agreement the conversation moved to less fraught subjects and we managed to part as friends. Later, I brought the matter up with Her Imperial Majesty when His Majesty was absent, but he had already told her about what I said, and despite pulling rank I got a frosty reception. 'Impossible nonsense,' she said, 'and please don't mention it again.' So that was that. I was annoyed at my failure to push the idea further, as it would have been the salvation of Russia. I decided not to tell Olga until she was older. And I already know about the time when Olga bravely brought the matter up, and her unfortunate lack of success."

Everybody was amazed at Brother Grigory's revelations, and there was a long silence while the listeners mulled over the ramifications and what might have been. Then Olga felt it was time somebody said something and that it was up to her to speak first. She was very upset, but dignified.

"Brother Grigory Efimovich, on behalf of myself and my country, I would like to state my gratitude for your brave attempts to gain for Russia the succession of a person who would have ruled her entirely for her own good, under God."

The other three felt what a scandal it was that Olga's spirituality and high motivation were going to be wasted. Olga went on:

"I have felt for years that my country is doomed, but in view of what Brother Grigory Efimovich has said, I now know there is nothing I can do to prevent it. It is almost as though His Imperial Majesty wants catastrophe for Russia. He cannot see the coming events, and even if he could see them he would do nothing. Despair is a sin, but it is also a logical reaction in this situation."

To Count Worthton she said,

"Monsieur le Comte, I thank you profoundly for your care for Russia, and I sense that you do much work behind the scenes for the good of all the nations."

Despair was choking her. Her chest was tight and she could not breathe. She had to stop talking. She looked at the count, and struggled to speak.

"Please, monsieur, on my knees I beg you, for some ideas, inspirations, anything. What can I do for Russia at this late stage? Don't tell me I have to sink into inaction. My father would say he was resigned to the Will of God, but it is not the Will of God that my country should be destroyed. The only reason why bad men triumph is because good men do nothing. The bad men are working hard to destroy Russia. I want to work equally hard to save Russia, but I can't because I don't know what to do, and anyway, my intuitive feeling is that we are all much too late. Do you agree, monsieur?"

"No, madam, I don't. Nothing is hopeless until after the event."

"Oh, you mean you anticipate disaster." Olga closed her eyes and let her shoulders slump.

"No, madam, I would not put it so strongly as that. 'Never give up' is a cliché, but a true one."

"So, very well, monsieur, I agree that I don't give up; but I might as well, because there is nothing that I can do."

"You can continue to pray."

"Monsieur le Comte, the effect of my puny prayers against the evil undermining Russia is like bailing out Lake Baikal with a teaspoon."

"Prayers always help, sometimes more than you expect, and in the most critical situations they may tip the balance. Another good thing you are already doing, is improving yourself so as to do your best in your station in life. Do not underestimate this, either."

In the face of the count's logic, Olga's emotions fought her common sense. She was torn between what she wanted to see for her country, and what she was seeing.

"It's no use," she thought. "In a minute he's going to end this meeting and all I've got out of it is a few minor ideas for later in my life, nothing at all for now. If a diplomat of his experience can't suggest anything it really is hopeless. And Brother Grigory is terrific but although he was respectful about my worries, which is more than you can say for Pappa and Mamma, he couldn't really suggest anything either.

"Over the years I've often contemplated killing Pappa and Mamma and Alexis and bagging the throne. I've always been serious about it, but now I am desperate. Maybe I should start doing, not just thinking. Could I dress up as a poor woman and attack them in the street? Get hold of poison somewhere, and put it in their food? No, I must not get caught. The key thing is to get myself on that throne and save this country from ruin," she thought.

The count said,

"All actions should obey the moral law. To sink to the level of the enemy is defeat, even if the world sees success."

Olga felt herself turning pink. How did he know she had been contemplating three murders as she sat there looking innocent? She looked at him. An electric current of blue flame came from his eyes and hit her forehead. She flinched, but it was pure uplifting spiritual energy and it gently cleared her despair. She began to understand that not all bad things could be cured, no matter how much she wanted them to be. "Very well," she resolved to herself, "I'll do what I can within my limitations. I'll improve myself, study and pray, and offer to God as a penance the fact that I have got to accept things I can't change."

The nightmare that the destruction of Russia might be a thing she could not change came to her, but it was too much, and she pushed it away. She would think about that subject again some other day.

Not much more was said that day. The count closed the meeting and the girls thanked him and Brother Grigory. Olga realised that her hopes of the meeting solving everything had been too high, but she was glad to have been in the presence of Count Worthton for that valued hour. She had gained spiritual strength from him and even though the situation was no better, she felt more able to handle things.

Olga and Tatiana, 1914

During the summer of 1914 Olga watched with hopeless fury as her country slid into the abyss of war and death. Brother Grigory Efimovich might have saved the situation, but he was in Siberia, recovering from an assassination attempt carried out, by a satanic coincidence, just at the time when he could have prevented wholesale catastrophe. He sent telegram after despairing telegram to Nicholas, telling him to keep out of war. But armaments men keen for profit pushed military men keen for glory to push Nicholas to fall into the clutches of the warmongers. He did, and Olga's life began to change in ways which she could not have imagined.

One day in late August Olga was feeling less oppressed with gloom than normal, because the Sun was shining and even though the war had broken out some weeks before, the two girls did not yet know the horrors to come. She breezed into the salon to find Tatiana slumped in a chair, looking glum.

"Hello there, Tatiana, what's new?"

Tatiana sat up. "I'll tell you what's new, me just realising that you are a bossy great interfering prattler, that's what's new."

Olga stopped walking and stared. "Me? You, well, I like that, I really do. Why shouldn't I wax bossy when I see fit? After all, I'm the eldest. I can't help it if being taller than me makes you think you can sit around all day giving orders and instructions to the entire universe."

"My growing taller than you was an accident of nature and you can't blame me for it. Marie's taller than you now as well, anyway."

"Tatiana, don't you ever realise that you're sometimes just too much?"

"Too much what?"

"Too good. Yes, now I've realised something. You, madam, are far too good for your own good, and for mine, and all of us. You keep trying to turn the rest of us girls into imitations of yourself, but you can't do that, we are not you, and it doesn't work. I'm really far less bossy than you, but I occasionally do resist your blandishments, proclamations, and-or threats when I think you're going too far. And because trying to run the family, the country and the world is so deeply ingrained into your character, you interpret the slightest squeak of protest as a full-scale revolution to be met and repulsed by all the heavy artillery you can dig up. You'd do well to get married to some nice young man who is supposed to rule a great big country but can't be bothered, and rule it for him, well, let's face it, like Mamma rules Russia for Pappa," Tatiana looked furious, but Olga kept going, "having a lovely time telling a hundred million people what to do all day, besides producing ten children and turning all of them into miniature Tatianas. Then you'd be fulfilled and happy."

Tatiana grunted. "You three all find me too bossy, do you? Well, I don't think I am too bossy. Everybody needs organising, including us girls."

"Oh, do be your age." Olga gave up, and wandered out, puzzled about what was annoying Tatiana. Well, she'd give her some time and space to help her recover. Olga went off and played the piano for an hour, then wondered if Tatiana was feeling better. She was just leaving the small piano room when they bumped into each other outside the door.

"Oops, crash, hello Tatiana, I was just coming to see how you were. Must have been telepathy."

"Hello, Olga, sorry I roared at you earlier. I was worried about the war."

"Oh well, it's not too bad at the moment, though I still think we shouldn't have got into it in the first place."

"You're telling me. And what do you think of Mamma's idea that you and I should train as nurses?"

"BLOODY horrible, if you ask me. What a come-down. I was hoping to find some nice tall handsome rich man and get married and get away from this place, which I am by now thoroughly fed up with despite all the luxury."

"You shouldn't be horrible about Mamma behind her back, Olga. She's your mother and she loves you."

"Look, Tatiana, I'm not in the mood for a fight. Life has got horribly serious in the past few months, what with that awful attack on Brother Grigory, and now the war engulfing us and virtually the whole of Europe. Gosh, I've had a thought."

"What?"

"Could Russia being pulled into the war, be a punishment for the attack on Brother Grigory? After all, to try and kill a holy man is a great crime isn't it."

"Olga, that is complete nonsense, out of all proportion. Can't you see that?"

"But it is a coincidence."

"Yes, it is a coincidence, and that's all it is, I assure you, big sister. Any other idea is pretty dismal theology. Think about it, Olga."

"Yes all right, Tattiboots Bossikins. You're not the only would-be theologian in the world."

"And if you think up any more insulting nicknames for me I'll…"

"Pull my hair and tear my dress and scream, like we used to," finished Olga helpfully. "No, I've just thought of that name and it's my best yet. Still, sorry I used it, I'll stick to Tatty in future."

The girls strolled along the wide corridor.

"Do you remember Ollikins when Pappa tried to stop the war? You shouldn't be so critical of him; after all, he is your father."

"Don't call me Ollikins, or I won't even threaten to call you Tattikins, and pull your hair and scream and tear your dress. This is all too serious for an orgy of name-calling. And don't preach at me so much. You're driving me up the wall. If I ever get to carve anything on your gravestone, I'm going to put, 'Her middle name was "Should"'. Yes, no, sorry, I really must get serious about all this. I do remember, very well indeed, Pappa trying to get Austria and Serbia together at The Hague, but it didn't work did it and we're all at war now. I suppose we all should have tried harder, maybe going on long fasts and difficult pilgrimages, or doing extra prayer sessions or something. People seem to want war, don't they? They say they want peace, but don't do anything to help it, and then they rush in in their thousands to join up when a war does start."

"Yes, and look how they cheered. I feel sorry for them. A frenzy of patriotism is so easy to create but once the armies are marching it's impossible to stop it all."

"I agree, Tatiana. And I am worried. I fear our generation will see the end of everything we value."

"Mmm?"

"Don't you?"

"No, honestly I don't, Olga. Though I am concerned about the soldiers, and their families, I can see you are remembering what Brother Grigory used to tell us. He certainly is wise. After all, he tried his hardest to encourage Pappa in preventing the war from spreading all over the world like it has, and I am deeply sorry that all the efforts of them both and of other people, ended in failure. And you know how awfully upset Mamma is, because she is in an impossible position and must feel very torn. She declares frequently that she has been a loyal Russian ever since marrying Pappa, but it is extra hard for her because of all the relations she has got in Germany, whom we are now fighting against."

"Yes, it's always been the same, Tatiana; you can talk to Mamma more deeply than I can."

"But you relate to Pappa better, so it balances out."

The girls arrived at a verandah door, and wandered out on to the lawn, enjoying the autumn sunlight. Even Olga, with her enhanced perception, barely knew that soon the hate-filled hurricane of war and revolution would devastate the beautiful environment around them, in which the best work of man's hands enhanced the innocent loving generosity of Mother Earth, and reduce the perfection to a wilderness.

The Prophecy Of The Two Herons, 1915

The elder girls trained as nurses while the younger pair went on with their lessons. At first more slowly, but then very fast, life became more difficult for everybody including the imperial family. Catherine Palace at Tsarskoe Selo, now a hospital, was always busy. One day, Brother Grigory turned up and Olga, who would do anything to get away from the nursing, suggested that at their next free hour she and Tatiana accompany him on a walk round out of doors, and Brother Grigory agreed, "Yes, a walk round the lake and a discussion, for old times' sake."

The girls, having been given permission by their mother, knocked off and the group set off as usual, down the slope, then along keeping the lake to their right, updating on family gossip and war news. Then they got near the place where members of the park's heron family liked to stand and fish. Olga loved the herons and hoped that they would see one close up.

It was late afternoon; the Sun was low, and there was pink light everywhere. It was rare to see two herons at the same time and place, but as the party approached, two that were standing in the shallows, rose from the lake in that wonderful, dignified way they have. Brother Grigory stopped. He stood rigid for a few minutes, watching the herons as they first circled and then sped off into the distance.

Olga always remembered the sight. It was odd, that trick of the light. There must have been a gap in the prevalent pink light, because one heron looked pink and the other plain pale grey even though the light should have been all pink or all white. Afterwards, discussing the walk, Olga and Tatiana wondered if Brother Grigory had done it himself by some spiritual force. They never did know. After some minutes, he spoke, and what he said was really frightening.

"Do you see those two herons, my children? One is red and one is white. Soon, light that is white and light that is red will clash in this, our country of Russia. Red force and white force, and the red will win.

"Guard yourselves well, my daughters, and pray for your country. Pray for your country, because she will need those prayers, from you and from all good people throughout the world who care about our beloved land of Russia.

"Well may you remember this day and this moment, Lady Olga and Lady Tatiana, when your humble brother in God, Brother Grigory Efimovich, saw into the world of future probabilities and warned you of the menace of the red light which is rising to consume your land and people before it attempts to consume and destroy all the whole world and eliminate the Holy Name of Christ from out of all the nations.

"Weep for Russia and weep for your brother, Grigory, your brother in God, because I will not be here to see this struggle of the red against the white. I will be assassinated a few months before the forces of the red gain the upper hand."

The little party stood there, and for Olga, it was one of the worst moments in several lives. She wanted to shout out, "But isn't there anything any of us can do to prevent all this?" But she was struck dumb.

Eventually Brother Grigory moved and the spell was broken.

"Do not ask me, my children, if there is anything you can do to prevent these events. It is very much too late now. The seeds for the coming evil were laid over many years. Look at your own family for the prime example of what has been going on. Your revered royal father, the chief cause of disaster..."

Olga grunted in agreement, and nodded; Tatiana looked shocked.

"...with too much attention to detail, inability to see the big picture, corruption by default, total devotion to his family while neglecting his big family, the nation, swayed too easily by those that happened to be with him at any particular time."

The girls were pink and subdued.

"Your mother, the empress, sitting for hours in that confounded boudoir of hers. The Mauve Boudoir! Infamous room! Why was she not out doing big works of mercy, or waving to those who had stood all night to see her? She turned her head away from her people, and yet she thought they loved her! It was madness. It was all sheer lunacy." Olga realised with a shock that he was talking about the imperial family in the past tense.

"And you, my dear young ladies, cannot avoid blame. You could and should have done more, and not obeyed your parents when you knew they were doing wrong. You took the easy way out. Obedience is a misunderstood virtue. When obeying orders which are right, you are doing right, but if you obey orders which are wrong, you are instantly wrong, and sometimes more wrong than person who is giving the order. Remember this."

The girls waited. Tatiana was always the bossy one, but Olga felt that Tatiana was waiting for her to speak first because she was the elder. Olga was bursting with questions, like, how can obedience be wrong if the authority of the person is legitimate? And the herons and what Brother Grigory said they portended. Was there really nothing that could be done? For a moment, Olga did think it would have been better for her country if someone had assassinated her father years ago, and almost wished she had done it herself. She asked about obedience, but Brother Grigory just repeated that if a person knowingly obeys a wrong order, they automatically become wrong themselves.

Then Tatiana, who had been biding her time, jumped in quickly, and asked about the herons and the red light and the coming trouble. "Surely there must be something we can do, for goodness' sake," she frowned.

Brother Grigory did not answer her immediately, but started by talking about prophecy.

"Oh, my dear children, prophecy is a scientific art. It is possible for prophets to be right, but it is also possible for them to be wrong, and this is because the future is not fixed."

Tatiana squeaked, "Oh!" Olga stayed quiet, biting her lip and wondering if there was any hope for Russia.

"Prophets can see things, yes, and frequently do, but the fact that things are seen does not mean they have to happen or that seeing them will make them happen.

"For example, if you see a child, wandering near a large cart with dangerous wheels, what may be prophesied? Either you watch and do nothing, and prophesy that the child will be hit by the cart. Or you take action to prevent catastrophe by rushing to the child and moving her away from the cart. This example shows how things foreseen can be varied, and variable. Do you understand?"

The girls chorused, "Yes, Brother Grigory," and then stayed quiet. He carried on,

"So, my children, what do you glean from this?"

Olga and Tatiana looked towards each other for inspiration, but Brother Grigory was between them so it didn't help. Then Olga had a kind of vision. What if this applies to religious prophecies as well, she thought, but as usual, dear little Tattikins' brain was quicker at finding the words.

"You've cited an example of a person making a simple, obvious prophecy of a small thing near at hand and then acting so that it becomes untrue. Do you mean that this principle could apply to big, long-term things too, like the prophecies of disaster for our country?"

Brother Grigory nodded.

"Yes, prophecies are only an indication. Take our beloved country of Russia. Now, of Russia, many have been the prophecies of doom, and these I deprecate, because what we expect tends to happen and most people believe that prophecies indicate a future which is fixed and cannot be changed. I even suspect, sometimes, that our country's enemies put out negative statements, to make the people expect evil happenings, so that being resigned to disaster, they lose their will and initiative, and make less effort to keep their country great and powerful."

Olga could feel Tatiana's thoughts were the same as hers. Great and powerful? Old Brother Grigory hasn't been keeping up with recent events, has he. She felt it was her turn.

"Brother Grigory, with respect, I don't agree that Russia is great and powerful, certainly not now, if indeed she ever was."

He said nothing, so she went on.

"We're losing men hand over fist in this dreadful war. We should never have got into the war, but it's too late now. The internal set-up of the country is a shambles. No trains means no food, and no fuel means we can't run trains to get fuel and food to where they're needed. Mamma, instead of acting like an empress and organising things on the large scale, fiddle-faddles around doing nursing work which any woman could do, and has even shoved us two into it against our will."

Tatiana squeaked indignantly, but Olga ignored her.

"I feel so wasted. Almost any woman can learn to do nursing, and I feel that we two should be helping to run the country, not acting as glorified laundry assistants. Honestly, Brother Grigory, it's dreadful being a woman.

"But I'm digressing. I started by saying that I think our poor country is heading for catastrophe, and there's nothing we can do to prevent it. Maybe Russia was great in the past, well, I suppose so, but those history stories we were taught may be more myth than truth."

"My dear Lady Olga, you are distressed, and rightly so. Let us go the long route back, and talk more. To return to the nature of prophecy. We discussed how some prophecies can be changed. But you see, don't you, that if a situation is allowed to get too bad, it becomes irreversible, and disaster does ensue. God is merciful, but only for a certain length of time, and then he has to stop being merciful and start being judgmental, letting the catastrophe run its course."

"You mean he runs out of patience, Brother Grigory?" asked Tatiana.

Brother Grigory threw his head back the way he used to and thought a bit, gazing at the sky and then at the ground.

"No, not exactly. God is infinitely full of perfect qualities and does not run out of anything. What happens is, in our world his goodness is limited, not by any lack in him, but by our capacity to receive his love and manifest it as he wills."

"So you mean, he can't hang about waiting for ever?"

"That is what I mean, my child."

Olga asked, "So if only poor old useless stupid Pappa had taken notice of the advice intelligent men of experience were trying to offer him twenty years ago, maybe God would have stepped in to prevent Russia having all this catastrophe now?"

"No, Olga, that's not quite what I mean. God couldn't have stepped in, as you put it, it's more subtle than that, but he would have poured his grace into the situation. He might have sent some wisdom to your father, or humility to your mother, or, sent an adviser who could really make your father change. Your father would still have been responsible, but we would not have seen this wholesale slide into disaster. It is our purpose to be God's regents in this world, especially when we are rich and powerful. But always remember that for each step we take towards him, he can and will take at least two towards us. He wants to take steps towards us, but he can't until we approach him first."

"And," asked Olga, "I suppose this applies to the spiritual life of a nation as well as of an individual?"

"Yes."

"But it's still too late for Russia now, isn't it," went on Olga, "I mean, if Pappa had led the nation properly and made us all get down on our knees and pray years ago, and if he'd granted civil rights to the masses, and if he'd got his act together and stopped allowing Mamma to run rings round him, always following her wrong advice, it would all have been so different, with no great disasters, and no wars."

"And no revolution."

"Revolution?" the girls exclaimed, "What revolution?"

"Ah, my children, I can hardly bear to tell you what I see."

Olga was stunned. Not more horrors for Russia? "Please, God, don't! If you must have Russian blood for the expiation of our nation's sins, kill me instead but spare my country," she prayed silently.

It was Tatiana who spoke.

"Oh, good heavens, Brother Grigory, is this one of your prophecies that can't be prevented because things have got too bad and gone too far?"

Brother Grigory shook his head and sighed, but Tatiana pressed him.

"Please, Brother Grigory, let us have some warning of what to expect, even if things have gone beyond reversing. We two women are two of the most important and sensible people in the whole Russian empire. Please tell us what you see."

Brother Grigory stopped walking. Olga and Tatiana stared at him. He stood silent again, and then, he decided to tell them.

"Your brother in God will be murdered. Shortly afterwards, your royal father's throne will be toppled. Because your mother is not by his side, he will agree to abdicate. This will be the beginning of the ends for you.

Because you will have several ends, each more diminishing than the last. Some of you will escape into exile, but the Romanov dynasty will end, and Russia will sink into a sea of blood and torture and death from which she will not lift her head for many generations.

"Alas for our beloved country. I can hardly bear to allow my vision to operate and show me our future. And even more, it grieves me to tell you of these things, my dear precious children in God."

The walk finished in silence. They returned to the palace hospital. Brother Gregory went home to St. Petersburg. The girls went back to work.

Olga, Mid-1915

By the time Olga had been nursing for six months she knew how bad things were for the men in the front line. Her sympathy was stirred, and she felt a surge of fury against the unseen forces causing the suffering.

"Why do they do it?" she thought angrily. "And why does Pappa, who says he is an absolute ruler, let himself be pushed about like a zombified robot? If he is so darned absolute, why doesn't he dig his toes in when the country is being pushed into catastrophe? He's absolute in the little things, but when it's a case of Russia tearing itself to pieces he can't or won't lift a finger. He simply is not in control. Well, we all know who thinks SHE is in charge, dear darling Mamma.

"It's over Mamma that I differ most from my otherwise adored little sister. Tatiana loves Mamma so much, but I don't, I'm afraid. Oh, I suppose there is some feeling there, but the myth that parents and children always madly LOVE EACH OTHER is just that, a myth, and I don't agree at all with it. After all, how can we all love each other? We're all going our own different ways. We do have a duty as human beings to be decent to one another, but it's different now that we've grown up.

"We're adults now. We can't all just carry on this unhealthy addiction, this kind of intense mental incest, for each other. It's as unhealthy as any other addiction, and because it's bad for us, it's harming the whole country.

"As the ruling family we are a microcosm of the country. What we do affects every one of our subjects, or, I'll dare to use the word even though Tatiana would shout at me if she heard it, 'Citizens'. Take Pappa, for instance. If he was dynamic; if he acted like a brave leader; if he made Mamma

111

shut up and obey him like a proper wife should, this would help the mental climate of the whole country.

"Men would feel that their 'Little Father under God' was being manly, and this would pour new clean manliness into the veins of millions of them. It would help reduce the power of socialists, liberals, revolutionaries, and other wreckers of society, because it would give people in authority new energy, and muzzle people like Mamma who shouldn't rule but do so because the people who should do, can't or won't or both.

"I like men to be men and act in a tough manly way. If there are any decent men left alive after this infernal satanic war is over and I actually manage to get married to one of them, I want someone who is manly. What do I mean by that? Firm and decisive. Compassionate, yes, but disciplined. Discipline is absolutely essential; without discipline, you're nothing; you're not fit to call yourself human."

But slowly Olga's mental state worsened. By the end of 1915 she was hopeless and demoralised. She was so depressed, that she closed down emotionally and pushed all the hatred and despair from around her, into herself. Because she did this, sucking in the bad emanations, the air around her felt cleaner to other people. They thought she had at last adjusted to nursing. She allowed them to think so, and laughed at their stupidity. She was proud too. "I won't let them see my sorrow and anger," she decided, "not even darling Tatiana. It's too deep. I'll sort it out myself." But of course she could not.

The minute when she decided to pull the evil into herself was crucial. She knew that she was doing wrong and that it was unfair to herself and to everyone else; to herself, because it was not her job to clean up everyone else's mental contamination, and to everyone else because she was doing their job for them.

It was not even as though she had proper holidays, to go off to somewhere pleasant and spend some time free from thoughts of war.

But she was already depressed, and desperate. Even while she knew she was doing wrong, she went ahead and did it. Not doing it would have plunged her into indecision, and indecision was the worst of all suffering.

When you suffer indecision there is no hope. If you act, you are wrong. If you do not act, you are wrong. Because everything you do is wrong, everything associated with you is wrong. Your negative attitude attracts negative things to you, you blame yourself for them, and finally you know that you are totally wrong.

Olga could not know how dangerous her decision was, even though she knew she was building up trouble. This worried her for three days, though she had already forgotten the decision. But it was not worth more suffering now to make easier a future which, she realised in a moment of insight, she hoped would never arrive.

After all, what was the point of it all?

For her there was no future.

Her beloved Russia was in ruins, and that was all she cared about.

For the millionth time she cursed being banned from the throne. She should be heir apparent, not doing work any peasant could do.

"Nursing," she swore angrily. "Who the hell cares? Bloody horrible job. Bloody and horrible job. Yes, I feel sorry for the wounded men and know that they need nursing care now, but if I had been empress, this benighted country would never have been at war in the first place. I would have prevented it somehow, even if I had had to instigate a few cases of judicious political assassination to get the worst of the warmongers permanently out of the way.

"I'd have ruled for the welfare of not just the rich and powerful, but everybody. My God, I must have been a terrible king or queen in a former life to have this frustration now. And even worse, watching an absolute idiot wreck the realm. And worse still, that useless idiot is my own father, whom I used to love, so help me, before I realised what a catastrophe he was. Love him? I'd like to kill him now, and wish somebody had killed him years ago, God forgive me for saying this. No, God, don't forgive me; kill me instead because if you do I'll go off to the other side somewhere and instead of wasting all day doing silly stupid nursing I'll pray hard for Russia to have peace.

"I wonder. Should I kill him now or is it too late for it to do any good?" Then she stopped, remembering. She had gone through this question before. And what had happened? It had been that time when Count Worthton and Brother Grigory talked with her and Tatiana about world affairs, and she had turned so pink when the count divined her thoughts about murdering her parents and told her bluntly that murder was wrong.

She was going round in circles again.

Russia was an oarless skiff, caught in the grip of a whirlpool. In it sat Olga and a hundred and thirty million other people, a few looking out and seeing their doom approaching, but most of them unknowing.

Olga's Nursing

Tatiana was a good girl but Olga sometimes found her too good, and nursing drove a real wedge between the two girls for the first time. Olga detested nursing, and while Tatiana, being Mother's Girl, did the work because Mamma said so, Olga went on sulking to herself.

"Mamma didn't try hard enough to keep us out of war. She was so keen to prove she is a loyal Russian and not loyal to Germany, that she made the emperor of Russia get caught up into this war against Germany. The war is killing off all our young men; how ever will their wives support themselves? Mamma is wicked, yet Tatiana still loves her. It's terrible. I used to love Tatiana so much, but now I don't know what's happened. I used not to mind her ordering me about, and I still don't, in some ways, but there is such a gulf between us now. I think she is wrong to admire Mamma so much! Mamma has been a catastrophe for Russia, with bad decision after bad decision, forced on Pappa. Of course it's his fault too. Men should tell their wives what to do, not the other way round, well I think so anyway, after all, it's more natural, because women are emotional and that's dangerous for decision-making. Seeing Mamma give Pappa the orders for year upon year has made me sick. Their marriage has been grotesque, parroting about their love while pushing their country over a cliff. What use is it, them having a good marriage, while millions of their subjects are living in squalor? It's almost enough to put me off wanting to bother with marriage, should there be any nice men left around when this crazy self-destructive war ever finishes."

Both girls got exhausted, hot, cold, worried, and worst of all, shocked by their close-up view of the carnage, and their nerves became permanently on edge. The more introspective Olga used to take her own anguish out on herself by brooding deeply, but inherently bossy Tatiana reacted to the stress the other way, by taking her stressed feelings out on those around her, the nearest of whom was Olga. The girls were pushed apart more than ever when Tatiana launched into lectures at Olga who she had decided was uncaring and selfish.

"Now listen, Olga, it's no use, this sulking. You simply cannot go on behaving like this. You're making Mamma look even more worried than she needs to." One evening after they had both knocked off much too late for common sense, Tatiana sat on the edge of her bed and gave Olga her best firm look, and commenced her lecture for the fiftieth time.

"Now listen yourself, twat, you jolly well get out of my hair once and for all. You are too bossy by half and I've had enough. It's not fair, Tatiana. I am not even minding now because I am older than you. I feel you're taking out anger on me just because I'm here. It's not my fault if—"

"What isn't your fault?" said Tatiana too loudly. "All right, if you're really the eldest, take more responsibility. All our lives you've leant on me, relying on me to give the orders, letting me run everything and do everything for Mamma while she's been seriously ill, and—"

"Now look, sister dear, do stop for a moment; better still, for several moments. I know you're not happy, but neither am I. More important still, neither is Mamma, nor darling useless silly Pappa away at the front, nor the two little girls, nor that sick useless little bastard brother of ours who reckons he's going to pinch my throne. But the most important thing is, Russia, this country of ours, is in absolute deathly agony."

That dizzy feeling surged through Olga; her heartbeat went suddenly much too fast and she couldn't breathe. She always felt like this when she thought of Russia, as though, when Russia suffered she suffered too. She leaned forward, her chest hurting, and pulled in a breath. Dimly she noticed Tatiana staring.

"I hope that sister of mine doesn't think I'm going to keel over," she thought, "no, on the contrary, it would jolly well serve her right and give her a good fright if I did." She went on out loud.

"Now listen, Tatiana. I'm older than you, I agree. But do face facts. Point number one is, we simply mustn't fight each other. Argue, yes. But whilst arguing, we must keep a sense of humour. Let's face it, neither you nor I is ever going to get married and have a normal life, are we. We've got no chance of that at all, because all the decent men are being killed off, well, especially the decent ones because they are the men who volunteer first and get closest to the fighting.

"But, I was talking about Russia. Your and my being deprived of husbands is just a symptom of the large picture, and we are no different, in that respect, from millions of other Russian women. I mean, fancy being poor and having your husband come back maimed and unable to work and support you. Think of all those poor men we've been looking after. Some of the stories they tell us are appalling. And the less rank they have got in the army, the worse off they will be if they ever do get back home."

Tatiana was hunched up, staring. Olga went on,

"And whose fault is it that we're at war? Really, to be absolutely truthful, and I can't bear to say it but I have to, to a very great extent it's darling Pappa's fault." Olga felt herself turning pink. Damn it, she detested blushing at her age.

"Look, Tatiana, Pappa didn't have to take Russia into this war, did he?

"So you're blaming Pappa for this whole war now, are you? That's historically inaccurate for a start, Olga, and you know it, and furthermore, you yourself commented ages ago that it was our emperor, our Pappa, who tried to get some of the other nations together to talk things over. Well, we all

117

know that it was their fault and not Pappa's that they took no notice and pushed ahead into a Europe-wide war regardless. Get your facts right, even if you can't show any loyalty to your emperor. Slandering him is treachery, Olga, and you know it. He is your emperor and your father and it is your duty to be loyal to him. He is one of the—"

"All right, all right, I know, sister dear, just what you are going to say next, yes, I know he is one of the holiest men ever to sit on the throne of Russia. I know that and you know that I know, so please don't go on at me about that particular point. But after all, he declared war on Germany. He didn't need to. He could have kept us out of the war."

"He didn't declare war on Germany, they declared it on us, so get your facts right, Olga. After that, all Pappa's generals were pressing him…"

"Exactly. His generals. They're his subjects, aren't they? He should have told them to take his orders and shut up or shove off. I still think it all could and should have been sorted out by diplomacy."

Olga ran out of steam. She was tired, her lower back was playing up from the heavy lifting that she had been doing every day for weeks, and she felt feverish. She had enough sense to realise that her judgement was affected. She yawned, and blinked at Tatiana.

"Look, Tatiana my old fruitcake, I vote we close down our political discussion for now and declare that it's time for bed. You know what Mamma is like if we're a second late on morning parade at her chosen hour of oh-blank-hundred hours, and I'm so knocked out that I'll never get up in time if I don't go to bed absolutely now."

Tatiana managed a watery smile.

"Okay, Ollikins my dear, you win. I don't know what on earth we both thought we were arguing about, but it seems to have simmered down. Oh, yes, it was about nursing. Well, why don't we just accept that we don't agree about it, after all, we don't both have to like it; let's just say that I like nursing and you don't, and that there's a difference of opinion between two intelligent young lady adults."

"That's a good idea, Tatiana." Olga was too tired to say any more. She collected her things and padded off to the women's washroom to get ready for bed.

Bugs

Olga soon got fed up again. She sat on her bed in the room she shared with Tatiana and sulked, clutching her veil.

"Bugs, too, honestly Tatiana, they are the most horrible things. For a while I didn't mind the filthy beasts, and thought I'd got used to them, but then suddenly there were millions and millions more of them everywhere…"

"Yes of course there were; it was because the weather got warmer so they've multiplied."

Olga wrapped her arms around her head and groaned.

"Oh for heaven's sake, I knew you'd say that. Tatiana, listen, don't beg the question. The fact that I loathe bugs, and the reason why there are more bugs, are two separate facts, not necessarily connected with each other even though they may seem to be to someone who does not know how to think clearly."

Tatiana took a breath, and seeing another lecture coming, Olga threw her veil on the floor, kicked it, and barged in first.

"And don't start going on at me for picking you up on a point of logic. I'm entitled to dislike bugs. Suddenly there were tons more and I just went berserk, honestly, I was ready to desert to get away from it all. One of these days, I'm going to sleep standing up to stop them walking all over me in droves with their beastly antennae waving and their millions of tiny little jaws going chomp, chomp, yummy, chomp chomp. I just can't stand the little horrors. Some of them bite, and I'm terrified that they're going to crawl into my ears and nose and eyes and mouth. If they start eating your brain, you can die slowly and in awful agony, after months spent going mad first."

She picked up her veil and tried to pull it to pieces.

"This damned thing. Symbol of gender-based degradation and servitude. As I was saying, those wretched filthy creatures will kill us all. Do you know, I read somewhere that there are four thousand cockroaches on Earth for each human being! And here we are, fighting each other like idiots in a silly war that's doing no good and will destroy all culture if we don't stop it. We ought to co-operate in a great war on bugs, instead of a totally lunatic war on other human beings. Well, I'm going on down to tea. Coming, Tatiana?"

"No I am not coming. And before you go, Grand Duchess Olga Nicolaeivna, I've got something to say to you, madam traitor."

Olga's jaw dropped.

"And do you know why I'm calling you a traitor? You're succouring His Imperial Majesty's enemies."

Tatiana stomped over and stood a yard from her sister.

"Pappa approved this war against Kaiser Wilhelm of Germany. You should back up your emperor and stop whingeing. War on bugs indeed, you do talk rubbish. If the soldiers heard you, everybody would find out that one of the daughters of the imperial house was a pacifist and a traitor, and there would be mayhem. Fancy the palace guard having to come and arrest one of us! And you'd have to be shot, to maintain discipline. After all, you're not just one of his daughters, you're enrolled as a nurse, tending His Imperial Majesty's injured soldiers."

Olga stood up and put her hands on Tatiana's shoulders. The sisters stared at each other.

Olga was exhausted, and upset at the endless fights with Tatiana. They had always had fights, but now that the fun had gone out of them there seemed to be no fun in life at all, and she felt heavy in spirit. She stared into the peculiar, timeless eyes of this strange sister of hers. Tatiana was eternal and wonderful, outside and above time, somehow. Olga felt again the awed stillness which came over her when she was with Tatiana. Her sister was a strange, wise, old soul, and maybe God had made them be in the same family so that they could teach each other. Well, Tatiana certainly taught her, but Olga could not fathom what she was supposed to be teaching Tatiana. She felt that her sister was worlds above and beyond her in wisdom and knowledge. She shook Tatiana's shoulders gently and winced at the hostility which the friendly gesture brought up on her face.

"Listen, Tatiana. Both you and I are sensible young ladies, and we know that we agree on all the basic principles. But I still think this war is wrong, shush, it's all right, I am talking quietly. It is wrong. Nearly all war is wrong; but just saying so doesn't make me a traitor. After all, I'm doing a war oriented job which is showing support for Pappa, even though secretly I don't agree with his getting into the war in the first place. It's wrecking the country, and that's my chief reason for being opposed to it. Millions of men are dying or being injured. And not a square yard of territory is being gained for all these deaths and injuries. But even if it was, I don't think territory is worth the life of one soldier, never mind thousands."

Olga sat down, and then she stood up again.

"Look, we'll miss tea, and then we'll be even more exhausted and fed up. Let's go and eat, and we can carry on talking afterwards if we feel we've really got to. Why don't we declare a truce for now, go to tea, and talk politics some time when we're not both crazy with exhaustion?" She pulled her veil to shape and put it back on, fiddling with it and trying not to pull angry faces.

Tatiana nodded gratefully, took a deep breath, and turned away to pick up her bag.

"Righto," she agreed, "fight over for now. And let's hope that there's some food left and we can get a decent tea."

"With no bugs in the food," added Olga.

The two sisters laughed and headed down the corridor to the distant dining room.

Olga and the Deva, 1916

Olga sank more and more into depression as the war went on. Brother Grigory's Prophecy of the Two Herons affected her badly. She forced herself to continue with regular prayers, but with a heavy heart, knowing that nothing could save Russia, and more from her innate respect for Count Worthton and his advice rather than because she thought any more that her prayers would make any difference.

By the late summer of 1916, the squalor, smells and suffering were destroying her spirit. Seeing the splendid rooms and grounds that she loved and had grown up in, become degraded and unkempt, wore her out and added to her exhaustion in a way that she never thought it could. She did not begrudge the men their hospital care, but it was all so unnecessary, because if only her father had been strong and kept Russia out of the war there would not have been these endless numbers of suffering injured men in the first place. She was tempted to criticise him to herself again, but decided that she had better things to do. She was so depressed that she could not even chat to Tatiana about her feelings any more.

One lunchtime she walked round the lake to the place where Brother Grigory made the prophecy about the herons and the two girls had stood there frozen in horror at his words. She stood there now, loathing the spot but unable to leave it, shuddering and remembering, and longing to be away from it all, anywhere, to some place or state where she would find peace, beauty and culture again instead of this endless stinking hell of men's bodies that had been torn apart in the most horrible cruel ways. She stared into the water, wanting to throw herself in but not daring to because of the old religious teaching dinned into her head as a child, "Suicide is a major sin!" Then she had a brainwave. How about suicide, killing herself not in a cowardly attempt to avoid her responsibilities and get away from it all, because that was impossible, but telling God first that she wanted to die to help Russia and offering her blood to him as a tiny bit of cleansing, in a deliberate, ritualised act of conscious self sacrifice?

"Should I?" she worried. "The church says suicide is a sin. Soldiers are not sinning when they go to certain death, but killing myself is different from that. Would God accept it as a sacrifice for Russia, or would he say killing oneself can never be justified by any motive and it was still the sin of suicide? Upsetting him would only make things worse.

"Brother Grigory said years ago that having one's blood spilled out over the ground by one's country's enemies was a very powerful act of magic, because it helps build up a wall of protection round the country. But would this still apply if I killed myself?

"Suppose I decided I wasn't wrong to do it. Should I still stay alive in the faith that a theoretical future lifetime of work is more help to Russia than one big positive act of sacrifice which is good at the time but whose effects will fade away? Once I'm dead I won't be able to help Russia very much, but it's now that Russia needs help. I don't mind dying. I just want to do what is best for my country.

"I won't mention this idea to Tatiana. She's too righteous, and would only get shocked and start ranting at me. She takes the Ten Commandments literally, whereas I'm far more flexible about them. She'd rush off and tell tales to Mamma, and I'd be locked up or something. I'll think and pray hard about it for a week, and then decide, saying I've got faith that God and his angels will guide me to do the right thing for this, my great country, Beloved Mother Russia, greatest country in the world."

Olga worked hard on her decision. She consulted her prayer books, and prayed to Saint Michael the Archangel, the great soldier, the greatest angel in Heaven, Commander of the Heavenly Host, Prince of God's armies, and Defeater of Satan. She had always been a great devotee of Saint Michael, and now she turned to him with her deepest and most determined devotion for his trustworthy love and support in this, the greatest decision she had ever made.

"Oh Saint Michael the Archangel! You love Russia and you love me, your little girl down here on Earth. Please see me kneel to you, and listen to my prayers. Bless me with the ability to see what is best for my beloved Russia, and to do it!"

On the fourth day of her week of extra prayer she remembered an exercise she had invented when she was thirteen, but had not done for a while, a curious kind of semi-spiritual exercise which just popped into her head one day not long after Brother Grigory had given her and Tatiana one of his lectures about Nature's forces. The exercise worked really well and she had never told anybody, even Tatiana, about it, and she decided that with her country being in such need of all the help she could give it, now was a good time for her to do the exercise again. On her next lunch break she sneaked off into the woods, and found one of her favourite retreats, a quiet, remote place where nobody else ever seemed to come. She lay flat on the ground, head to the north, arms out, feet together. She relaxed and breathed deeply. She willed herself to become a figure in the landscape. In her vision the edges of her body blurred, then disappeared.

She became one with Russia. She knew its past, present and future. Magnetic energy flowed to her from the farthest reaches of the Russian lands. She willed it into herself, filled it with pure love from her breath, and then sent it out to flow in steady waves across the land. Spots of light sprang up as it came to holy places on route. She loved her country so much, she felt light-headed. Then that passed, and she was steady again. An existence free from the normal boundaries of time and space was hers. She was Russia, she herself was her country, and was helping to create its continued existence by breathing its past into herself, purifying that past, and breathing it out in a spiritualised state to become the country's present and future.

Something told her to get up. Slowly she did so, and felt impressed to sit cross-legged, facing east, with her hands resting on her knees. Still in the mild trance state, she felt a presence come down round her, a presence which was vibrantly alive, invisible, yet seen by her mind's eye, a four-sided pyramid eight feet square and five feet high, deep grey in colour. In answer to her devotion, the living being came, and communicated by thought to Olga that he was willing to work with her, manipulating Russia's energies, if she wished. Intuitively she knew that this was the Great National Deva of Russia, guardian spirit of her country in the Devic Kingdom.

Awed and joyful, Olga sat still. Here was the opportunity of many lifetimes. This Deva Master was totally identified with Russia, and if she could communicate with him, she could gain wisdom and learn more about how to help Russia. Olga wanted to sing with excitement, but she realised that she must stay calm. She wanted to do so much. Forcing her mind to go cold and logical, she prayed for inspiration and rapidly formulated questions to put to the Deva Master.

First, would he please let her see the country the way he saw it. She was willing to wait indefinitely for his answer, but did not have to because her mind was instantly lifted miles high up into the air. She gazed down in wonder as beneath her lay Russia, spread out like a living map perfect in every detail, like the maps she had studied years ago in class but this time glowing with internal fire and more alive than she could ever have imagined. Rays of gold and white light were flowing from her down over the land, like a cloud of protection.

"Oh, wonderful," she thought. "I've always wanted this."

"How do I help my country most?" she went on.

"Prayer, devotion, love and work." The words flowed down into the top of her head.

Olga thought for a minute. Now she must ask her important personal question.

"Would it help Russia if I killed myself and made my blood be poured out over the ground in a rite of sacrifice?" She fired out the thought with all the power of her mind, forcing herself to know that a definite, helpful answer would come to her.

There was a silence, and Olga assumed that the Deva Master was thinking about her question. Then she was physically shaken, just like in an earthquake, and a huge voice from all round her shouted just one word,

"No!"

And there was silence again.

Olga hung there in the sky, looking down at Russia spread out below. Very well, she would stay alive, and pray and work hard.

"Thank you, Oh God, for making your mighty Deva Master tell me that you don't want me to kill myself as a sacrifice for my beloved country of Russia," she thought politely. She felt a bit peeved. Her brainwave was not so brilliant after all. But never mind, this process she was doing was terrific and exciting, and she would do as she had originally planned and complete her week of extra prayer anyway, to show Holy God that she kept her word.

Next, she would see if she could find out what dangers Russia faced, and looked down with interest to see how much of that sort of information was available to her in this visionary state. The map, or some force in charge of it, reacted to her unspoken request, and she saw, far to the west and south-west, the enemy lines where her country's soldiers were fighting for survival. Moscow and St. Petersburg were surrounded by pale haze. "I wonder what that means," she thought, but could not work it out, and decided that it was not important enough to ask the Deva Master about it; she ought to be able to interpret her own visions herself. Then she looked to the south-east, at the great mountain ranges. She had never been there herself, but knew them all from the maps she had studied in class, and was interested to see that her attention was being drawn to the great range of Pamir.

Pamir! She thrilled to the name. When they were little, one of their nurses had regaled them with tales of big woolly lambs who lived with their mummy and daddy sheep on the slopes of the Pamir range; they were the biggest sheep in the world, with wonderful thick wool and big curly horns, the nurse had assured the intent little girls. Olga smiled at the memory. She requested a nearer view. Straight away she felt she was five miles above the range, and she stared down at the snowy wonderland. She saw the physical mountains, but also, to her surprise, the lines of geomantic energy.

"Brother Grigory talked about those energies," she thought, "and how Mount Pamir is an important centre of them, and how vital they are to human and plant life. He told me I'd see them one day. I am certainly seeing them now, although I never imagined that I'd be seeing them in this way, so when I get the chance I'll tell him he was right. Let's see, there's a huge line flowing northwards, one due eastwards, and one south-westwards. Funny how I can see them even though they're below the surface. They look like silvery rivers."

She looked a bit more, then felt it was time to return to duty. She let go of the vision of Pamir, and hovered once again high above Russia. She requested "return", and saw a thin silver cord reaching from her, down to her body. There was a jolt, and she blinked. She was sitting stiff and frozen in the familiar woods. The pyramid-shaped Deva Master had departed, and she was alone. For a moment she sat still, reviewing the experience and coming back down to Earth again.

"The Great National Deva of Russia," she said to herself. "I've worked with him. How marvellous. I do hope I'll work with him again. Thank you, oh God, for enabling me to do this for my country of Russia. And thank you, Saint Michael the Archangel, for answering my prayers so spectacularly."

She got up and rubbed her limbs to get warm. "Good heavens, the Sun has gone round and I'm going to be really late back. Mamma will be hopping mad and I do hope she won't start a big to-do about where on earth have I been, or start ranting that I'm setting a bad example to the other nurses because as I am a member of the imperial family they look up to me for an example, blah blah blah, well, hard luck if she does. I'll say I went for a walk, sat down for a rest, and nodded off, which is more or less true, and she will jolly well have to put up with that much. After all, she can't complain too much about me nodding off because we are all always exhausted and she knows that. I've been saved from suicide by God's mercy, and helped Russia in a great spiritual way, so if I'm late back on duty to her filthy stupid nursing it's too bad. What I've done today is infinitely more good for Russia than if I'd spent a year slogging at Dear Mamma's pestilential nursing."

She returned to the palace enjoying the early autumn colours of the trees and deciding that if she ever wrote her memoirs in some dim future time when the war was over, this episode would form an interesting and central chapter in the story. Memoirs, she cogitated, well, maybe, sometime. Who knows.

The First End

After working with the Great National Deva of Russia, Olga felt better, but she knew that the cataclysm was close. In mid December 1916 the first part of Brother Grigory's prophecy came true, when his murder caused shock to the imperial family and joy to the many who had seen him as either an arrogant upstart or a subversive influence or both. Feeling intuitively that with his spiritual protection of the country being ended, Russia was now hopelessly vulnerable, Olga knew that the end had come. She was beyond despair now, and had retreated completely into a shell from which she looked out at a world from which she began more and more to retreat, even while putting on a brave face to fool people around her and keep them from asking interfering if well-meaning questions.

With their natural immunity reduced by the stresses of the years of war, the five imperial children all fell victim to sickness at the same time. Their mother Alexandra, sensitive, overworked and well-meaning, became unable to see the wood from the trees, turned away from running the country, and closely supervised the children's care herself. She should have paid a nurse, and given attention to her husband, who was now under hopeless stress and pressure due to war and incipient revolution, and though doing his best with great and genuine effort, could not cope. Olga drifted in a fever, too ill to note events. No longer protected by Brother Grigory, and without Alexandra by his side to assist him, Nicholas gave in to the pressures and agreed to abdicate, on 15th March 1917. Alexandra was shattered when she heard, but knew that it was to a great extent her fault. In a moment of insight, she saw how her gross straying from God's law for years on end had brought all this catastrophe about. The son she had plotted and schemed for, centre of her life's ambition, would now never rule Russia, even for a short time. But it was too late. She had plenty of time now to regret being absent from Nicholas's side when he needed her most, and even worse, at one of the rare moments in their lives when her influence over him would have been for the good.

Revolutionaries took over nearby St. Petersburg and marched on Tsarskoe Selo. Alexandra's staff begged her to leave, but she refused, saying the children were ill. A few hours later the railway lines were cut and her chance to get the family away was gone.

Nicholas was brought back, as plain Citizen Romanov.

Rudge did a session of psychic viewing and noted with pleasure the state of Nicholas and Alexandra as they met each other shortly afterwards. "Two of history's greatest failures, and aware of it; serves that Nikolay right for humiliating me all those years ago!" he recorded with glee in his Magical Diary.

At first the family members and some staff were confined in Tsarskoe Selo, in relative comfort. In August 1917 the moderate socialist leader Kerensky had them moved to Tobolsk, three hundred miles east of the Urals, in western Siberia; for greater safety, some said. In November 1917 the left-wing "bolsheviks", dedicated communists, took over and life became much harder almost overnight. Olga gave up thinking about the causes of it all, because the imperial family had enough to do trying to survive. Then in early 1918, in two groups separated by just under a month, they were moved to Ekaterinburg, back nearer the Urals.

Ekaterinburg was the worst possible place for them to be sent; it was full of angry workers who wanted revenge against the man whose family they blamed for the sufferings of the centuries, and who they claimed was personally responsible for all their miseries over the past two decades. The Romanovs were getting near the final one of the series of

"Ends" forecast by Brother Grigory Efimovich. Olga was in the second group, who arrived, after a trip by boat and train, on 22nd May 1918.

The house loomed in front of them, pale cream, and ornate but dingy. Olga shivered, feeling that she was arriving at a meeting with her ultimate fate. She surveyed the empty windows, but saw no familiar faces and wondered if they were at the back; she did not yet know that the prisoners, her family, were forbidden to look outside. Of course it was raining. Olga splashed through puddles, and muttered angrily as the water leaked into her shoes. She turned round, and saw Tatiana frowning up at the building with an apprehensive look on her face. The girls did not speak, for fear of a clout from a guard, but a look from one to the other said a lot these days. "This looks a right dump we've arrived at."

"Come on you ruddy lot of useless imperial layabouts, move it, we friends of the people aren't going to hang around all day for your convenience," bawled a large fellow, aiming a clout at Tatiana, who ducked, looking furious but not daring to protest. Olga frowned, and went to help her sister with the big suitcase.

Round the house was a big wooden fence; it was high and featureless, noticed Olga quickly, so no good for a quick climb over to get out. "Heaven help us," she thought, "We're going to have a right job and a half to get out of this lot. It's a pity we didn't make some bids when we were first locked up, the country was a complete shambles, and we might have walked out more easily." The guard, a big, scruffy man dressed in a mixture of old army wear and stolen civilian finery, fumbled with the large keys. Olga quickly put on her best innocent expression while noting where the guard kept the keys, but they hung on his belt, which was no use at all; she would not be able to steal them easily and walk out.

The guard opened the gate and Olga picked up her bag. An assortment of other unkempt guards, probably self-appointed she guessed, roared rude comments as the little group of prisoners went in, but Olga took no notice. She took one look round, and went cold all over. "I don't believe it," she thought, "there's a second damned blasted fence inside that first one, and I'll bet it goes all around the house as well." She took a deep breath, and noted the positioning of everything carefully as they went through the second fence. Inside, close up, the house looked even worse than it had from a distance. It had obviously been beautifully built originally, but as usual the bolsheviks had wrecked what they could out of "revenge" against people of her class. "I bet it's damp and freezing," she thought, "and those perishing guards will have stolen all the carpets and curtains and things, to teach us one of their silly stupid so-called 'lessons', leaving us with nothing as usual; what absolute rats they are, and we've very little warm gear with us for next winter." A part of her mind dared to add to herself, "If we haven't got the heck out of this blasted hole and off to freedom somewhere before winter."

The entrance smelt of cold mossy stone. The head guard banged on the door and it creaked open to reveal more uncouth guards who were clearly waiting for the imperial family to arrive. As Olga walked in, a short, stocky man bowed mockingly. Olga wished he would bang his head on the floor, but no such luck. The prisoners came to a halt in the hall, and stood waiting. One of the indoor guards signed a paper, which Olga guessed was a receipt, and the escort left. Olga couldn't hear any familiar voices, and wondered again where the rest of the family were. For the thousandth time she resigned herself. She was hungry and wet, and felt a mess, and was worried about everyone else. "Poor old Tatiana," she thought. "Look how thin she is, and she's still got that dreadful cough. I hope to God it isn't tuberculosis, but we'll have to wait and see. Oh, damn all this waiting and seeing. I wish I could be in charge of my own life again for just one minute occasionally; one of these days I shall scream."

She recited a short prayer and felt better, but knowing that if the situation itself was not altered, just feeling better did not help her much. For a moment, a mental picture of Count Worthton, that cultured man of another era, swam into view in her mind, and she remembered his words, "Prayer can sometimes make more difference than you might expect"; well, she had better keep her prayers up now because there was nothing much else that was going to help them.

Nicholas, Alexandra, Marie and some staff had been in the Ekaterinburg house for nearly a month. After greeting the members of his family, Nicholas made a point of speaking to the servants who had also just arrived. Bowing to the Romanovs was now punished, but they still saw Nicholas as their master and greeted him warmly. All of the prisoners were worried about each other. Tatiana went to Alexandra, murmured "Darling Mamma", and gave her a long, gentle hug. Olga, uptight as ever, found it hard to look her father in the eye but gave him a dutiful hug and then marched over to Marie.

"Hello, poppet, what have things been like here for you since we last met?"

"Not too bad, Olga, but my goodness it is good to have you here." Marie was whispering, and looked pale and distraught. Olga guessed that being the oldest family girl in the house for a month had told on her, what with trying to help her mother in her poor health, and, like the gentle little soul that she was, no doubt putting her own sufferings aside in an attempt to cheer and support their father as well. After all, Marie was still just a girl, and imprisonment had shocked her and little Anastasia much worse than it affected Olga and Tatiana who were older and had grown tougher thanks to their years of nursing.

Olga was so angry with her father, and felt that all the catastrophe was his fault.

"After all," she remembered for the thousandth time, "he was always saying he was an absolute ruler and felt responsible; well, that makes him the one person who is most responsible. If only he had run the country properly, and listened to the endless warnings from people who tried to tell him how wrong things were going. If I am ever a ruler in a future life, I am somehow going to make sure that I remember all this debacle and handle things in a totally different way. For a start, I will not trust what courtiers tell me, especially when they say that things are going well, but I will get out there and listen to the people, not to a shower of idiots who daren't tell me the truth. I will get proper professional advisors in, people like Count Worthton who was dead straight and told the truth regardless and got disliked for his pains. I'll have a proper staff team and pay them all a straight salary; none of this gifts nonsense which leads to corruption. Then I'll listen to what they have to say about their own specialist subjects. Hell's bells, here I am, at twenty-two, and I know more about how to run an empire than that father of mine ever did. Some emperor!"

Again she cursed the foul fate of being a woman, and the idiotic ban on women instituted by that insane, hateful ancestor of theirs. If only she'd been a man, that useless little twat Alexis would never have been born and she would be successor, her mother's health would not have been worn out trying to produce a son, and then, instead of locking themselves away to protect Alexis, her parents would have been out and about, providing leadership and inspiration to show that they cared.

God! A hundred and thirty million citizens, she refused to say "subjects" any more, and what did they do? Hide themselves away and ignore upheavals, with Mamma still thinking that the four girls believed the people loved her! But Olga had talked in depth with the fighting men in her hospital days and had heard how life was for the poor men and women in the endless remote villages. A hell in life. Olga wondered for a moment why people inflicted such dreadful

135

experiences on themselves, but then shrugged and gave up on the question, feeling it was beyond her.

Her thoughts raced on furiously, banging against the walls of her anger and frustration, feeling personal, deep sorrow for the very old people, the young, the little babies, who were all of them suffering because of her father's ineptitude. It was a pity that the assassination attempt a few years ago didn't succeed, she frowned. It might have improved things by getting Alexis in as nominal ruler while the country was run by one of the other, adult Grand Dukes, most of whom, she thought sourly, were far more capable than Nicholas would be for three more lives. Now, it was all too late and nothing could make a difference any more to the fate of her country.

Olga's old love for her father had drained out of her feet into the endless pit of judgement. "Judge not and you won't be judged," someone had said, Aristotle was it, she couldn't remember and anyway it did not matter. "But when I have seen the physical results of complete cruel stupidity, I feel entitled to judge, when my country is in agony," she thought, as she watched the others, feeling completely cut off from them as she secretly did all the time, now. And the chief failure, that man whom she now loathed with all her soul, in his tatty uniform, with his sunken cheeks, his blue eyes too patient and too submissive, was her own father. How she had grown away from him. She realised that she had just wished him dead, and was glad because it meant that at last she was her own woman and free of her parents. Now, she thought as she took a deep breath, she really didn't mind dying, oh no, wait a minute, she did mind dying because she wanted to stay alive for as long as possible to help her country, her beloved Russia.

"Have a good journey?" Nicholas was saying. Olga did not feel able to be civil. Luckily, dear old Tatiana replied, "Satisfactory, thank you, Pappa," while Olga stood there glowering. Alexandra glanced at her anxiously. Olga caught the look and did not care. Marie, kind and motherly as ever, put her arm round Olga's waist and Olga unwound a little. "Thank goodness little sister didn't tell me to cheer up," she thought, "or I would have thumped her."

Marie was the first to divine that Olga was going to have a nervous breakdown, and even in her own suffering, she made time to try and help big sister stay sane. It didn't work, but Olga was always grateful for her efforts.

"Come and see your new home, Olga, it's not that bad, honestly." Olga just made a face, but Marie steered her down the corridor to a doorway where they stopped. Olga blinked in dismay at the tiny room, with four beds, narrow cupboards, a couple of chairs, and not even a table. And why was the window shut, were the bolsheviks trying to kill them off? Olga gasped in horror and dismay, but then her religious faith surfaced and she blessed herself, muttering "God help us." Marie stood quietly, her arm around Olga's waist, willing her courage.

Then Olga noticed why the window looked odd. My God, it was whitewashed. Yes, the bolsheviks must be trying to drive them all stark raving mad: no blue sky, no trees, no view? No fresh air was bad enough, but the thought of never seeing again the blue of God's dwelling in heaven, the friendly twinkly stars at night, or the peaceful moon? For one moment, Olga knew that for her, this was the last of the Ends forecast by Brother Grigory, and that she was certainly doomed, and that this bedroom would be the last place where she would regularly come to take her rest at night. Then, mercifully, that knowledge was taken away again from her conscious remembering mind, and she was left feeling drained. A warm hug from Marie revived her, although she was never the same from then on, because a bit more life had gone out of her with that brief realisation of her coming end.

Marie said, "Mamma and Pappa and Alexis are down the corridor, and the staff who are left."

"Well, I don't think much of this lot. What a dump. Oops," Olga gasped as her arm was seized, and turned her head to see, sneering down at her, a large guard with two more behind him. She tried not to shrink away.

"Now then my poppet, there's no need to make ungrateful remarks about your living conditions. All of you will live in that there room and like it, see? You enemies of the people are going to learn what suffering your inept uncaring stupidity and criminal greed has brought upon us, the great Russian people. See? You've lived well while we lived in hell. Ho ho, I didn't know I was a poet! Hey, Georgi," he roared to a colleague down the corridor, "listen to this, I'm a poet. These useless swabs have lived well while the people lived in hell. What do you reckon to that, eh?"

Olga was staring up at him with a mixture of fury and apprehension.

"Didn't think you were going to come down in the world to this, did you, MISS useless little layabout Romanov? Well, you'll learn here what life is like for working men and women, and I'll bet it's the first time you've ever worked, eh? Whoo-hoo, you didn't like that," he crowed as Olga frowned. He clouted her round the shoulders, nearly knocking her flying, and the three men strode off.

Olga took a deep breath and opened her mouth to comment. "Shsh," said Marie before she could explode, "I know it's awful, Olga my dear, but you'll just have to get used to it like we already have over the past three weeks. The guards make us spend a lot of the time doing menial jobs which they invent on the spur of the moment; also we study and pray and read together, and sew, partly to keep busy but mainly to stop our clothes falling to pieces, because of course we never get any new clothes now. There's only a little money to maintain us and the servants, oops, we're not allowed to use the word 'servants', and it's important to remember that because the guards just go totally mad if you say it. You have to use the expression, 'our valued staff colleagues'." Olga's face was a picture. "All the money that's made available for us goes on food, and that's not brilliant either."

Marie stopped and fixed Olga with a solemn look.

"I know it's awful, Olga darling, but at least we're together again and we are still all right."

"All right? What in the hell use is that?" snarled Olga, in shock after the past half hour. Marie merely gave her another hug, and Olga nearly threw her down the corridor. Then she calmed down, and allowed Marie to steer her back to the big room, where she noticed guards milling about and getting in the way. "When are those guards going to clear off and leave us in peace?" she murmured.

Marie gasped. "They wander about as they please, and if they think you're complaining, they'll steal everybody's food as a punishment, and it's if they think you are that counts, not, whether you really are or not. Honestly, Olga dear, you'll have to remember to guard your tongue."

Olga was indeed in shock. From being a royal grand duchess, with her life mapped out, she had become a war nurse and seen mass suffering. At the revolution her father abdicated and she lost her position, titles and future. Imprisonment at Tsarskoe Selo had been bad enough, then Tobolsk, and now she was stuck in this dump. How much worse could things get? But her anger dissolved because part of her agreed with the guard. It was true that her family had lived well while a large percentage of the Russian people were suffering. And that father of hers had led them into war, she said to herself, knowing that she was getting her history wrong but not caring, and his rule of her country had ended in civil strife, famine, and epidemics. "Well," Olga cogitated, "maybe we Romanovs are getting what we deserve."

Clearly Almighty God wanted her to be a part of her family's repentance for the suffering which they had caused to Russia. She resolved to be positive and make the best of things, and for a while, what was left of her courage and fortitude kept her able to function.

Days At Ekaterinburg, 1918

Olga sighed as she stretched and woke, spinning it out to the last second. She never wanted to wake now. She was beyond depression. Her emotions were deep and harrowing, but were locked in her head. There was nothing to live and express emotion for. Even her hatred of her father was dulled. She would never, never, never, forgive him for the destruction of her beloved Russia, but at present, she had decided, she would just not think about him any more.

The guards were everywhere, and she and the other girls had no peace. They had worked out a method of dressing in a little group together, so that if a guard barged in they could shield each other. There was no lock on the bathroom door, so they went in pairs. Taking a bath was next to impossible, because the water was only hot when the guards felt generous. Olga had always liked to bath every day, but now, she shivered at the thought and revelled in the warmth of her blankets for another minute, knowing that she would have to move soon.

Crash! came a loud and no doubt unnecessary noise from outside the room, and Olga groaned. "There they go again," she thought. "Why do they have to make such a racket?" Feet clumped heavily up the corridor and the four girls gasped as three guards barged in.

"Here you are me beauties, here's your morning tea, and bread, and eggs with lashings of butter. Eat up." Olga winced at the thought of all those wonderful foods which they never saw any more. The guards stood together in the centre of the room, leering round at the girls. There was silence for a moment, then they turned and marched out again, banging the door so hard that a piece of plaster fell down from the wall.

"Good God, this is a complete madhouse," thought Olga.

Marie sat up bravely, trying to look cheerful.

"Right, ladies, it's time to get up," she announced, "and don't forget to sample the wonderful breakfast our valued staff colleague guards have just brought in!"

"Don't be a prat," Tatiana growled, and Olga glanced over towards her, feeling anxious. Her beloved bossyboots of a sister was not her usual self. Olga sighed and looked round, thinking she had better get used to all this, because it was the way things were now. She got out of bed, and went and sat on Tatiana's bed. All she could see was a mop of untidy hair.

"Tatiana, darling, are you feeling all right?" she said softly. She knew her sister well enough to sit and wait. A flushed face appeared, and Olga swallowed when she saw how awfully thin and feverish Tatiana looked. Tatiana coughed painfully and muttered, "'Scuse me." She yawned and then launched into pretending that she was still her old managerial self. "Right, girls, welcome to the delights of another day at Ekaterinburg Hotel Splendide. Let's get up before the heavy squad come and try to help us get dressed. It's my and Olga's turn to get the water. Come on, big sister, where's the bowl?"

Olga sighed. This was typical Tatiana, valiant little thing, always ready to ginger up the rest of the prisoners.

A guard was slouching in a padded chair outside the door. He stuck out his foot and Tatiana managed not to fall over it, which would have brought shouts of how this degenerate enemy of the people had arrogantly and deliberately attacked a long-suffering Russian comrade by kicking his foot, and deserved some dire punishment. The guard called out rude remarks as the girls went down the corridor, filled the bowl, and came back. They were forbidden to close the bedroom door themselves, or he would wrench it open and issue punishment, so Olga and Tatiana left it half open, pulling a face at each other and hoping he would stay put in his chair for the next ten minutes. He did this time, and the four girls managed to wash and dress in peace.

The next adventure was lunch. It was usually stale meat, thin gravy, a few potatoes or other root vegetables, and occasionally, gritty bread; but there were no fresh greens, and butter had almost faded in their memories. There was plenty of water to drink provided that the supply was on, and tea arrived in fits and starts. Sometimes local nuns brought in dairy produce, but a lot of it was stolen on its way to the Romanovs. The guards left the door of their ground floor kitchen open so that the Romanovs were taunted by delicious smells. The family's meals were prepared by the faithful young cook who had stayed with them. He was "helped" by the guards, who stole what they liked. Olga wondered why the guards did not make them cook their own food, but this would mean giving the Romanovs access to food supplies, and the guards did not want to do that.

Olga wondered why they still bothered with a written menu. The reality never came anywhere near to the optimistic description; but still, they had let enough things slip, so it was good for their morale to keep up appearances when they could.

And what ought they to do about clothes? They did their best, but everything got slowly more battered and worn. It was summer now, but they had to get better clothes by October or they would be dangerously short when winter arrived. They had got only one real set of clothes each, plus a few spare items. Could they steal clothes from the guards, she wondered. That would be difficult, and, anyway, the things would be seen, and a severe punishment was certain for the offence of theft. They could make up some garments out of blankets, but they only had a few and needed them for sleeping, especially in winter, when she was sure there would be no heating.

As usual, Olga said a silent prayer. It may not improve things, but if her mind was peaceful she had more chance of coming up with solutions.

Memories And Thoughts

One late afternoon the prisoners were in the salon. Nicholas was in his favourite chair, with his feet resting on a stool, and Alexandra was slouched in her wheelchair, sewing. Olga was reading for the hundredth time one of the books they had still got, and the other three girls were sewing. Alexis lay quietly on a couch; he looked feverish, Olga noted, and felt sorry for him, even regretting for a tenth of a second her long-standing anger at his old right to the throne which she had always felt should have been hers. "Poor little thing," she thought, "he never had a chance." She remembered the scene at Tsarskoe Selo when Alexis was told that their father had abdicated in his name as well as his own. He screamed, a horrible high-pitched noise. Nicholas had been hundreds of miles away, but Alexis raved as though to his face.

"You should have given me the opportunity. You had no right to take away my opportunity. I would have tried to do something for my beloved Russia, my country, my only love. I would have had your useless example to avoid. How dare you do this to me. Kings have succeeded at the age of ten. I am fourteen. You call me a man. Now you have taken my manhood away, and I am nothing. You are a complete failure. You plotted and took drugs to have a son, and named me successor. Now you deprive me of my position. From now on I have nothing to live for."

And he rushed out, unable to face the sad faces of his family and the fearful embarrassment of the servants. He wandered off for an hour, and when he came back, no one had the nerve to say anything to him about it all.

Olga sighed. If only that daft ancestor of theirs had not stripped women of their right to the throne. Typical bloody

Romanov. She looked back over their history. "Three hundred years on, the country is a shambles and the people have risen in despair at our uselessness," she thought. "Well, I don't altogether agree with them, but I hope that the revolutionaries can do a better job than us lot ever did."

"Penny for your thoughts, Olga," came Tatiana's musical voice.

Olga jumped, and nearly dropped her book. She nodded that she was back in the room again, and smiled at her sister.

"Mmm," she said vaguely. How she loathed being cramped up. In their previous life, she and Tatiana had terrific discussions. They would put the world to rights over a good pot of tea, arguing with the depth and ferocity of people who feel deeply at ease with each other, the verbal equivalent, she thought fondly, of the fights they used to have when they were little, screaming, pulling each other's hair, calling each other "Tatty" and "Olly", and even tearing each other's dresses when they got really carried away. Some of her first sewing lessons had been on partially dismembered dresses. What a thing it had been, to be innocent and young, not knowing what was coming to them later.

"You've been a naughty girl again and torn your nice kind sister Tatiana's dress, Olga," Miss Andreas, their nurse, would say solemnly. "And so your mother the empress says you have to repair it, so come on now and be a good girl. If you tear, you have to repair; if you fight, you are not right; no pulling hair, because that's not fair. You're a good, cultured young lady, not a tough little boy."

And Olga would fume, thinking that if those silly rhymes were poetry, then poetry must be jolly boring, and the last thing she wanted to be was a "good girl". And why should she repair Tatiana's dress? Tatiana was too bossy already. Mend Tatiana's dress indeed. Well, Olga would make sure that Tatiana mended Olga's dress too, which of course did happen, because Miss Andreas meted out penalties and rewards with complete fairness. The girls had loved and respected her, and Olga wondered where she was now. She had left under a cloud when the girls were still young. Olga gleaned from friendly servants that the empress sacked Miss Andreas for complaining about Brother Grigory, which could be true, Olga had to admit, because plenty of people had criticised him and been rewarded with the sack. Olga liked Brother Grigory when they were young, although later on, she began to wonder whether the rumours could be true. Some of the newspapers had been really scathing about him, but maybe the man visiting low class houses in St. Petersburg was a double, paid by his enemies to bring the real Brother Grigory into disrepute.

Could the truth be somewhere in the middle? From her own many meetings with him, and the amount that she had learned from him, she could never believe he was the "devil" figure of the newspaper writers, but she had to admit he'd had a lot of influence on her parents. But then, what was wrong with them, trying to do their best in their important, lonely and lifelong job, selecting an advisor whom they wanted and continually found helpful? But, again, maybe it was odd, how he had wandered out of the backwoods of Siberia and into the palace, with not much formal education, nor diplomatic experience, although he certainly knew a lot, and had helped her and the other children by talking with them about religion, nature and current affairs.

Well, poor Brother Grigory was dead now, thanks to those horrible cousins. It was a shame somebody didn't finish them off, and she hoped that one day somebody would, because they deserved it for murdering a holy man, regardless of how seditious they thought he was. Olga felt they had been jealous of his influence, after all, he couldn't have been evil, look at the way he had tried to keep Nicholas out of war. By one of those terrible blows of fate, he had been away sick in Siberia, recovering from injuries inflicted by a would-be assassin. If only he had been with Nicholas, the emperor might have kept Russia out of the war under the full strength of Brother Grigory's terrific personality, in that awful, deadly summer of 1914.

"Tea's ready," chirruped Anastasia, who had been working busily, and Olga yawned and looked round. She would have to stop reminiscing for now, and go to help the other girls get the invalids organised. They all sat down and tried to enjoy another meal of leftover soldiers' rations from the barracks across the road.

And so life dragged on.

Another day, Tatiana said, "Penny for them, Olga."

"Mmm; I was just thinking about Germany."

"You're joking; what do you want to think about them for?" Tatiana gave her sister a reproachful look.

"No, seriously. When we were young we didn't think of them as enemies, did we; after all, we've got lots of cousins over there, and we liked and respected Germany."

"Well, you were always better at German than me. Maybe you've got more natural sympathy for them."

"Well, yes, there's that, but in a more general sense, think of all the things that Germany has given to civilisation, like Bach, Beethoven, Goethe, and many other important big names, and their scientific and engineering ability. It's dreadful that we ended up fighting against a nation that's given so many splendid things to the world."

Tatiana kicked a chairleg. "We Russians have given splendid things to the world, didn't you remember? Come on Olga, that's sedition you're talking. Get patriotic and stop succouring your emperor's enemies."

"Tatiana, you must have been an inquisitionist sometime in a recent past life. You really know how to press all the right buttons to make me angry, don't you. All I do is state a view, and if you don't like it you start to rant like a bad-tempered sergeant major on a parade ground."

"I – DO – NOT – RANT!!! You're the limit, Olga. Why shouldn't I have an opinion? You are usually the patriotic one. What's happened to you these days, do I have to start teaching you your basic lessons?"

Nicholas looked at Olga, worried. Recently she had been behaving strangely, staring at him fixedly while looking as though her thoughts were elsewhere. But, he noted with relief, Tatiana looked as sensible as ever; no doubt she'd keep Olga's spirits up. Olga went on.

"Tatiana, I don't know what's gone wrong with both of us. Do you remember, we used to have terrific talks about world affairs, but yet not be fighting just discussing? Don't tell me we've fallen out." By now Alexandra was listening, while Marie and Anastasia were pretending to carry on sewing.

"No, Olga darling, we haven't fallen out but let's get things into perspective. We're living in reduced circumstances, we have no privacy, those dear 'valued comrade guards' spy on us, oops sorry, supervise us, all the time, we don't have the food we're used to, and we don't even have nice things like a good hairdo. Never mind any new clothes. Now, take a deep breath and stop looking so tragic, no, I mean it, take a breath in, nice and deep, that's it; and let it go out slowly, and now another, the same again. And move your shoulders and shake your hands a bit. Honestly, I promise I'm not laughing at you. Deep breath. There, that's better, isn't it. You look better too.

"As I was saying. Deprivation can do all sorts of things, like, make people short-tempered and liable to fly off the handle. If we remember what's happening, I'm sure we'll be able to carry on having good discussions without fighting each other."

"Mmm, I hope so." The stuffy air made Olga sleepy. Grateful for Tatiana's common sense, she went on reading her book even though she knew it almost off by heart, and slowly managed to doze off to sleep.

Escape Talk

Olga liked to sneak away to the empty room near the back stairs, to peer out at the real world through a little scratch she had made in the whitewash on the window pane. Glimpsing normal people out there on the road helped her to stay sane. Early one afternoon, in the summer of 1918, she was staring out longingly when instinct warned her to turn round, and she had just leapt guiltily away from the window when Vladimir, one of the guards, walked in. Olga bit her lip. He was alone, instead of in a group of three as they were always supposed to be, so what was he up to? Should she yell for help? But then the guards might question her about what she was doing in the room on her own and she was afraid she might confess to looking out of the window, upon which the whole family would be severely punished. She stood frozen as the man walked towards her, but then everything changed as he said words which she had never thought she would hear again.

"My Lady Olga," and Olga gasped, suddenly feeling hopeful when she heard him use the forbidden title. "Lady Olga," he said, again, as though to reassure her, "two of us guards here are loyal to His Imperial Majesty, and to his family, and we want to help as many as possible of you to escape from this awful place. I am approaching you, my lady, as the eldest of the young ones, to ask if you are willing to trust me and the one other guard who I know is loyal too. Will you take risks, and obey what we say immediately without any questions, no matter how mad it seems? Are you willing to keep silent about this whole idea, and tell no one in your family, not even His Imperial Majesty, unless or until I say you can?"

"I, er, yes we'll obey you, but why can't we... that is to say, I... don't you want the emperor to escape as well?" Olga stuttered, in shock, and nervous that someone else might come along the corridor outside and interrupt the conversation. She stared hard into Vladimir's eyes, trying to assess whether to trust him or not, but in a way not caring anyway. By now she was willing to contemplate risks which she would not have considered a year ago. So what if they died escaping? It would be better to take a risk and follow up any offer of help, than to sit here like fools any longer. The family were never going to get out of this place courtesy of the bolsheviks, that was certain.

"Their Imperial Majesties are too tightly guarded and the Tsarevich is too ill, and so that leaves you four ladies who may be able, not only to get out of here, but to make the long journey afterwards too. I ask you, my Lady Olga, to approach the other ladies, and that you decide among yourselves how many of you four will join in. I will approach you again in one week, but meantime, take care not to speak to me in any way, or to recognise me more than usual. Start getting clothes and shoes ready for a long journey, and remember that if any escape talk is overheard you will all, and your servants, be executed out of hand, without trial, immediately. Farewell for now and God bless you."

Vladimir turned quickly and left, leaving Olga standing, taking a deep breath and trying to gather her wits together. Friendly guards? Escape? Thanks be to God, their situation was not hopeless after all. So, now what should she do, and the old remedy came to mind: when in doubt, have a cautious word with Tatiana. Good old Miss Bossyboots, the Managing Director, was the only person to approach about a matter as important as this. She stood still for a moment, glaring at the door and then at the floor, muttering imprecations against the guards and other looters who had stolen all the carpets. Footsteps and chat carried far and easily in the stripped, bare rooms, so she and the other girls would have to be incredibly careful about where and when to talk, or even how they walked around, from now on. They would have to check up on things like squeaky floorboards, and remember to avoid them, she decided, and headed for the door. Feeling she could face anything now that there was hope, she trotted quietly back to the salon, looking innocent, and sat down to pretend to read.

Two days later at Sunday divine service Olga sat by Tatiana, and pointed to the words "must" and "speak together" in her prayer book. Tatiana nodded and the girls resumed looking devoted, although Olga's thoughts did a lot of escaping and not much praying.

Back in the salon after worship, Tatiana fussed over Alexandra as she always did, organising her sewing and her glasses of tea and water. From behind Alexandra's head, she · winked at Olga, who nodded, went to the door of the room, and peered out into the corridor. A few yards away, by the top of the main staircase, sat the usual guard, an elderly, surly man, who always sat dozing over his newspaper until the main troop came back after lunch-hour. He only appeared on Sundays, so the Romanovs had nicknamed him "Sunday" among themselves. Olga stood looking innocent, Tatiana finished helping her mother and joined Olga, and the two girls headed down the corridor towards the bathroom.

They glanced back, and noted that "Sunday" was asleep, with his newspaper all over the floor beside him. They scooted past the bathroom and dived into the big end room, and Tatiana pushed the door nearly shut.

"What is it, Olga?"

"Tatiana! You know Vladimir, the guard, one of those three that do a long day shift on Tuesdays and Fridays? Well, the day before yesterday he found me alone in here and I was scared stiff and thought he'd caught me looking out of the window, but he hadn't seen me do that and anyway, he said that he and another guard are loyal and want to help us to escape. Just us girls, not the others, because of their health and the travelling and so on. We're to decide who is coming, and he'll approach me again next Friday, and in the meantime we are to get clothes and shoes ready for a long and difficult journey. But the thing I didn't like was, he said we mustn't tell Mamma and Pappa and also, er, if we're heard talking about escape at all, we'll be, er, shot without trial at once. So, what do you think, Tatiana, do you think that we should trust him and make the effort?"

Tatiana had been watching the door as she listened to Olga and thought quickly about all the implications, and now she nodded firmly.

"Yes, I think we should. Let's face it, we won't survive if all we do is sit here. We've been locked up now for well over a year and if those dumb monarchist groups were ever going to get us out of here, they would have by now. As you know, all the stupid clowns bloody well do is fight each other for the honour of rescuing us. With friends like that who needs enemies? No, let's go for it, big sister. I vote it's far better to die trying than wait to be shot by these murderous bolshies. And of course we can't tell our sainted parents. Don't you remember what happened last time we came up with a plan, and the pair of them went berserk and said No, and stamped on the plan, almost as though we'd been criminals for making the suggestion, and if only we had ignored them we would have got away? No, Olga. Just remember what Pappa used to din into us when we were little, and not so little, that our first duty is to Russia. Well, I'm afraid we're going to do what he said, and put our duty to Russia first, and leave him here to sweat it out. It is far better for our country if some of us stay here and get shot than if everybody stays here and gets shot."

"Tatiana, you've made a good point, but..." Olga hesitated, "We're condemning our parents to death."

"Olga! How do you think I like having to think like this, and say such things? Can't you see this is the last chance for any remnant of our family to survive at all? For heaven's sake back me up or I'll start wavering. If some of us can make it to Great Britain, or to anywhere that's safe, we could help Russia. We might set up a free government in exile, or write books and letters, or give lectures to tell everybody what is really going on, and so on. Anything! Try to see the broad picture, of what's good for Russia."

Tatiana's instinctively spoken appeal to Olga's patriotism won.

"Yes, you're right, Tatiana. I'm with you and I agree that we should join the enterprise wholeheartedly." She could not bear to think about poor darling Pappa and Mamma and little Alexis, being left here to be killed by those awful bolsheviks, and bit her lip to stop herself upsetting Tatiana by mentioning them again. She took a deep breath and went on.

"Now, what about the Little Pair? I think maybe Anastasia is too young to be trusted to keep such a secret?"

"They must both have the chance to get out, but I agree that we can't trust Anastasia to keep a thing as important as this secret for possibly weeks on end. You know what she's like. I'll ask Marie, and let you know before next Friday. But I'll leave asking Anastasia until the day before, and then what we say will have to depend on what Vladimir feels is safe anyway. She only has to forget herself and blab it out with her big mouth, and we'd be absolutely finished, literally. Look Olga, this is all marvellous, but we can't talk here for too long, or someone will notice and start asking awkward questions. Let's go back to the others via the bathroom so they think that's where we've been. Chins up, big sister, and do remember to keep happy, but don't suddenly start to look happy or people will want to know why."

They returned to the rest of their family in the salon.

"Oh there you are," said Nicholas, "I do wish you two girls wouldn't wander off like that. You can't trust these guards."

"No, Pappa, sorry," Olga said quickly, hoping this would pacify her father and praying that neither he nor her mother would notice how flustered she must be looking. She picked up her book and pretended to read. Her heart was beating like mad and her head hurt. She hoped that she would be fit enough to escape and walk for thousands of miles through desolate forests and hostile workers. Then she checked herself, realising that thinking about escape was unwise in case she forgot the need for absolute secrecy and blurted out something that gave it all away. She would work on the clothes, but no more than normal in case someone noticed and asked her what she needed them for now it was summer. She frowned down at her book, and tried to forget escape for a bit and focus on reading the story, to give her head a rest.

Olga's Dream

By the middle of June 1918 the escape was set for two weeks' time and the three eldest girls, especially Olga, were feeling the tension of pretending to look normal while they prepared clothes and tried to get fitter. Vladimir had introduced them to the other loyal guard, Mikhail, so that they would know whom to trust on escape night. He passed information to the little group through Olga, who manfully learned his instructions by heart and then whispered them to Tatiana and Marie when they could sneak away for five minutes' occasional privacy.

One afternoon the imperial family were, as ever, sitting around confined in the big communal room. Marie and Anastasia had gone off to the bathroom, Nicholas was reading to Alexandra, who was sewing, and Alexis was lying flat to conserve what strength he had got left, his eyes shut as he too listened to his father's voice. The air was desperately stuffy as usual, and Olga, who needed huge amounts of oxygen to function properly, felt really light-headed with her head tight and her eyes shutting all the time. She was worried that she was going mad. She was trying to read, but was getting that feeling which she was getting more and more now, of being pulled away backwards from the room. Was it madness, or a heart attack? She was not afraid of dying, and she almost wanted to die because she was so worn down by the horrors which Russia was suffering while she was forced to sit useless, unable to help her beloved adored country, the only thing in the universe that she cared about. A spark of loyalty to Russia kept her forcing herself to keep asking God to help her to live and be brave.

"Never want to die!" Brother Grigory had said to her and Tatiana one day in 1913 while they were discussing death and what happens after it. Olga had felt guilty as his eyes bored into hers, and did not know why, then, but now, she realised he must have been seeing into her future, here in Ekaterinburg, divined her mental state, and been trying to warn her.

"While there is life there is always hope." Coming from anyone else it would have been a cliché, but Olga could take it without resentment when Brother Grigory said it.

Now, she repeated the words to herself and rubbed her head with her hands, but it did not work and her vision began to fade again.

"Olga, have you got a headache?" Tatiana picked up her chair and came and sat beside her. She took Olga's hand and massaged it.

"Uh, thanks Tatiana, I feel so weird, like, my eyes are fading, fading away, I can't focus, my brain and my eyes aren't connecting up, I need more air, I can't breathe," Olga rambled on. Then her pet theme came to mind and she started her usual diatribe.

"Bloody Romanovs, all of us, useless crap rubbish, deserve to be tortured and shot for our failure. Look at him," she pointed to Nicholas, "Citizen Romanov, can't even be a decent citizen. No wonder he got thrown out, he was always drugged, on opium, all his life, and the rumours were right. They should turn him into a worker, yes, to work would do him good, real work, down a mine or in a stoke-hold or in a field trying to grow food for his eleven children that he can't feed. He should try living in a hovel, in a hovel like his policies condemned millions of his people to. We are all pathetic garbage, all of us. In my next life, I hope that I am a real worker, a proper worker, not a silly useless ornament being bought and sold into some dreadful marriage for political gain. I want to do something useful somewhere sometime. God help me, I'm exhausted. Why don't they just shoot all of us and get it over with? We're all useless, not just him, Citizen Romanov, but all of us." She could see her father look pained and her mother look furious, but was beyond caring how anyone reacted.

Tatiana looked concerned. She had at long last experienced enough suffering herself not to attack Olga for feeling depressed, so for a moment she sat silent and just rubbed Olga's hand, moving the fingers in circles.

"Hold on Olga," she said quietly.

Olga tried to smile, but could only manage a horrible grimace. She slumped sideways and shut her eyes. Dimly she remembered, what was that important thing, oh yes, in two weeks' time they were supposed to escape. She almost laughed out loud. Maybe the others would get out, but she would not, it was too late now. Her brain was too scrambled to function, think, and remember. No. There was no escape for her. She couldn't cope any more, but she would put on a brave face and pretend to join in, until the others had got away safely. She didn't really want to leave Russia anyway. She couldn't bear to leave it and would prefer to die. She must arrange to be killed in a way which would spread her blood out over the ground, a good magical practice, someone once said, it must have been Brother Grigory; it helps to protect the land, he had told the two girls.

Besides, she felt that the Great National Deva of Russia would want her here, alive and free, helping him with magical manipulations of energy, like she had done that time in the forest shortly before the catastrophe. But when she was dead, would she be able to work with him any more? No, probably not; at least, she didn't feel certain that she would be able to. Oh, damn it, this meant that it was her duty to try and stay alive. Olga sighed, then smiled as she realised Tatiana would never know what she had been thinking. She opened her eyes, and her sister's pale face, large forehead, and concerned expression, met her. The girls gazed at each other, and then Olga felt ashamed of wanting to die. Tatiana had been through the same imprisonment, but wasn't sitting around ranting and whingeing. Once again, her younger sister's ancient grey eyes and inherent spirituality brought Olga back to life.

"Thank you, Tatiana," she said, feeling better. Tatiana shook her hand, but held on to it. Olga felt suddenly so sleepy that she realised with relief she could get to sleep now and forget everything for a little while. She closed her eyes, and nodded off despite the lumpy chair.

While she was asleep, her soul wandered away south-eastwards, and she was drawn to a Buddhist temple among high mountains. There she was delighted to meet an old friend. Count Worthton again, how wonderful, she said to herself, as she went to greet him. The count greeted her kindly and in the cool silence of the ancient wooden building he spoke to her, of the continuity of life, of her value to the universe, and how she had a right to exist and take her place in the web of existence.

"Life will support you, Olga, but you need just to relax and let it do so. Try not to fight the universe so much. Let it send help to you and accept the help instead of rebelling against it and pushing it away, which you are somewhat inclined to do out of a mixture of false and excessive independence, and a feeling that you don't deserve anything. If God sends you something, it must be because you deserve it, no matter how wonderful and beautiful it is. You do deserve it, truly." He paused, and then changed the subject.

"I have called you here today to give you some warning that you may have to die from the physical level soon. But rest assured, Olga, that if indeed this does happen, I and my colleagues here will organise help for you and those of your group who die too; you will all be met after you have passed on, and given the type of help which is best suited to the spiritual development of each of you.

"Olga, death is different from what people commonly think. It is not terrifying or dreadful, but is more like stepping through a doorway and finding yourself in a new country. That is all.

"Now, return to your body, Olga. I and my colleagues thank you for your tremendous devotion to your beloved country of Russia, and assure you that your prayers and sufferings for Her have gone up to the Throne of God and will be considered and answered. I know that you, and your excellent and noble sister Tatiana, and myself, will meet again when God wills it, and discourse on matters of great import to the world. For now, farewell, and may you have peace, and understanding."

Olga did not know why she joined her hands in front of her and bowed to the count, but it felt right. The temple faded and she floated away, to rest in a cool grey fog, experiencing no weight, no sound, and no view, until she blanked out entirely for a while.

She opened her eyes. Tatiana was still holding her hand, and the room was looking the same as ever. Olga felt as though she had been asleep for hours, but it did not matter. What a nice dream that had been, meeting the eminent count like that. He had said that she might die soon, but Olga suddenly decided that she did not mind at all. If the count had said that, it was very likely to happen, so why was she not afraid, she wondered, and could not work it out. Well, she hoped that her death would help Russia; that was the main thing. Olga suddenly felt much better. She smiled at Tatiana and detached her hand. Her wonderful sister had given her such healing, but she didn't need any more at the moment. Not if she was going to die soon, she giggled to herself. Tatiana smiled back at her, looking relieved. Olga stretched and wiggled her toes, and decided to do something practical which would help everybody else. She would help Mamma more with the endless sewing, or take more turns at reading out loud. She was feeling better now than she had done for months.

Loyal Plotters

Leonid, Dmitri and Victor sat in Victor's flat in a back street of Ekaterinburg. The air was close in the small living room of faded yellow paint, threadbare rug and low ceiling. The men drank tea, puffed on cigarettes, and plotted.

"Right," said Leonid. "We've got to finalise plans because Theodor's heard the plane is getting near. We want anyone that does get out of the house, to be at his field to meet it. First, how many prisoners will we have to transport? Romanovs, I mean, as I don't feel that the servants are at risk."

"They are, guv'nor," said Victor. "The reds are vicious to people they call working class who refuse to join them."

"The imperial family have to take priority. I'd love to get all the seven family and four servants out, but they're really tightly guarded now and some are ill. In any case, it's said Nicholas has sworn never to leave Russia, and I doubt he'd leave Alexandra and the lad. So we've got to discount them. If we'd got artillery to knock a hole in the wall, and a battalion to get them away, oh, yes. But we haven't. There's us three, and Theodor's in contact with the house guards and the plane, and luckily he's still got a lorry and some fuel, and that's it. The four girls are all we can manage."

"Funny how they're willing to leave their parents."

"Maybe, but I hear the family have fallen out recently. There's talk of fights, of the eldest girl telling Nicholas he's bloody useless and has run the country into the ground. I feel the girls have given up and decided to get out and help Russia from abroad, start a resistance in exile maybe. Better than sitting about till they're shot by the bolsheviks."

"You've said it, guv'nor."

"Theodor's two men in the house are going to bring in extra hooch and start a party. They're going to get their mates tipsy and then start a fire. Yes, the ultimate cliché. They've got to get the upstairs guards away from that back staircase. While everyone is rolling about singing and panicking the girls have to get downstairs, which they're forbidden to do except at exercise times, and out of the back door, and out the gaps in the fences. Theodor will have his lorry there just before midnight, and the girls will leave at half minute intervals starting at midnight, and Theodor will drive off with what girls get out, leaving the house men to close the gaps and clean up any footprints."

"How will the girls know it's midnight?" asked Dmitri.

"I've been told that not all the Romanovs' stuff has been stolen, so either they've still got a watch, or our men will fix something."

"How will our men unlock the back door?" asked Victor.

"One of them is getting a copy of the key, don't ask me how, about now. He'll unlock the door, then lock it after the girls have left."

"And Theodor drives the escapers to my house to hide in the cellar," went on Dmitri.

"Yes, then gets himself straight out of town and heads for his farm by back roads."

"Why doesn't he just take the girls out then?"

"The curfew! It means there's far too much chance of being stopped. If he was found with the girls, just about all Ekaterinburg would be executed, but if he's stopped on his own, well, he's been pretending to be a loyal communist, so he'll brazen it out somehow."

"How about petrol?"

"He's been collecting it for months, and says he's got enough."

"All jolly dodgy, guv'nor. And how long will the young women be in my cellar?"

"Until the hoo-ha dies down; with luck, under a week."

"Hang on a minute, the bolshies are bound to execute the ones that don't get out, hasn't anyone thought about that?" protested Victor.

"Look my friend, when the entire country is on its last legs, it's better that some of the imperial family get away than none at all. The girls think so, and it's their own parents they're leaving. All is unfair in love and war."

The First Flight

Lieutenant William Reynolds was assistant to Major Jeremy Tierney, a long-serving and highly respected officer in the British Army, and the men had worked together since before the war. "Nelsonian" jobs, the boss liked to say, meaning that if the job which they did went all right they were both still alive at the end of it and the government collected all the honour and glory, but if the job didn't work out, they weren't, and the government didn't know anything about the affair. However, they were men of honour, and accepted the cards that life dealt them with humour and initiative.

William was pleased to hear that a Russia job was coming up, as it would give him a chance to practise his Russian again. The men sailed from Scotland to Murmansk on a ship full of British troops, and made their way to Tobolsk. On route they acquired an aeroplane from a Russian army contact, but then the Romanovs were moved again.

"Well, such is life," commented his boss, "but thank heavens we know where they are, so we'll go towards Ekaterinburg next. You know our old contact Theodor who owns a farm fifty miles from the town; I know his property and feel sure he'll be able to hide our plane on it somewhere, and then we'll decide on our next step."

Some days later, it was early morning, and William peered down from the aeroplane. The air was cold, he was cold, and everything was cold. "Heavens," he mused, "if it's like this in June, perish the thought of what it must be like here in winter. How on earth do people live here and survive the climate year in year out, they must be as tough as nails." The engine noise went quieter, meaning that the boss was planning his descent and landing. Finding the field had been easier than William hoped. They were five minutes early, and would not need to rush. William hoped and prayed that Theodor had got to the field. So far things had gone all right, but this meeting, and, he hoped, picking up any Romanovs who were hidden there, was by far the most dangerous bit. Theodor was keeping hidden, but by the south-western hedge lay the two parallel fallen trees which William had been looking out for. The slight early morning mist was just right; it showed Major Tierney that the air was still, but would not obscure his view as he made the final approach to land.

The engine went quiet, and they were committed to landing now. William had complete trust in Major Tierney's flying skills, but a million things could still go wrong. Of all the jobs of his six years' army service, this crazy venture of flying into territory occupied by manic groups all tearing each other apart, and all hostile to them as well as to each other, to pick up some people who may or may not even be anywhere near, was the most ludicrously optimistic, but, he appreciated, important in his boss's superiors' view. William peered down, and saw nothing moving on the ground. All he could hear was the swish of air along the outside of the slowly moving aircraft.

The wheels touched ground gently, the aircraft bounced slightly twice, and then the tailwheel dropped to the ground and acted as a brake, slowing the aircraft down. William kept up his alert lookout all round them. They were lucky that Theodor had a large flat field. The boss used the aircraft's impetus to steer, and stopped the aircraft twenty yards from the trees. William stood up slowly, and was pleased that everything was dead still, which meant they had not been seen by any roving bolshevik troops.

After a couple of minutes a man popped up behind the fallen trees. "Hooray," thought William, "Theodor has made it." Theodor waved, and ran to the aircraft.

"Hello, boss, well done. Let's get her out of sight."

"'Morning, Theodor, good to see you. You know my assistant Reynolds of course. Right, where can we put her?"

"She'll do under the big trees."

The three men manhandled the aircraft the few yards into cover, parked her with her nose outwards and her tail in a gap, and covered her with the matching branches which Theodor had picked ready.

"She shouldn't be seen in here, boss," said Theodor, "unless the fighting flows this way, and from what we've been seeing, I don't think it will in the next week or two. I've plenty of fuel, been collecting it for a long time now, and I'm glad it'll be useful for the cause. I've some hot tea here," and he rummaged in his jacket, producing a bottle of brown liquid which William eyed with interest. They sat down on a convenient log and enjoyed their tea, passing the bottle round in the absence of cups, but William noted with apprehension that Theodor looked worried, and wondered what sort of news was coming.

"Boss, I'm afraid it's bad news about the family. We've only got some of the girls lined up to get out."

"Oh? Lined up? I thought they were all supposed to be out by now, and ready for us to transport. Seven people, some of whom are ill, are going to take us all our time to get to any sort of safety. What's going on?"

"We've tried hard, but it's been far tougher than we feared. You know our three previous tries didn't work out, due mainly to those damned fool monarchist groups who can't co-operate, spend their time fighting each other instead of the enemy, and actively oppose any British or other foreign rescue attempts. With friends like that the imperial family don't need anyone else as enemies." Having made his favourite complaint heard, Theodor paused for breath.

"We've managed to keep track of the family, and as you know they are now in Ekaterinburg. They're in a big house right in the town. The set-up is this. They're kept upstairs and aren't allowed out except for a short time each day. There are two sets of guards, one lot in the house and the other in the garden, and they keep to their own areas. The family are very tightly watched. They have the rooms along the upstairs corridor. There's a main staircase at one end, and a small narrow stairs at the other. The rooms are big and open; there's nowhere to hide and also there are continual searches whenever the guards feel in the mood, day or night. There are guards inside and outside the two doors into the garden. The front door leads out from a big hallway, and the side one from a narrow corridor. The house guards go round in groups of three.

"We've got one man among the house guards, and one who's well in with the garden group. That's how we've found out all this. The garden is patrolled by ten men, who keep watch on a variable shift pattern that depends largely on how much alcohol they've drunk. There are two substantial stockades of wood planks right round the house, the inner one near the walls and touching at one corner, and going up as high as the first floor windows. The outer one is nearly as high, and from ten to thirty yards further out. The garden flower beds have long since been trodden flat and the whole garden is mud, which is hard or soft according to the weather, with a bit of thin grass.

"The salon, where the prisoners spend daytime, is by the main staircase, which is wide and open. Next is the room of Nicholas, Alexandra and Alexis, and they're locked up in it at night. Yes, we must not mention their titles, it's far too dangerous, so just use their names. Next is the four girls' room, but it's left unlocked. In the next room, the one remaining woman servant, and in the last room their doctor and two men servants. Beyond that are the two toilets, and the bathroom. Last is an empty room, big and echoing, which isn't used for anything at present. The carpets and most curtains were looted when the bolsheviks took over the house from its owner, one Nicholas Ipatiev, an engineer, in April, and no carpets means that footsteps and voices sound through the floors, so moving round at night must be kept to a minimum.

"Our man approached Olga, the eldest girl. She had a discussion with Tatiana, the next one, and they are preparing warm clothes etcetera. Our man says that he's made sure they understand the risks, and he persuaded them that they must not tell their parents by saying the locking up at night made it impossible to get everybody out. Olga sided with him, saying Nicholas insists the family are not split up, but has also sworn never to leave Russia, so it sounds as though he wants them all to sit and be shot with him, which I'm afraid is typical of the silly sod, sorry, but even though I'm a loyal imperialist I've had to recognise that that's all he is. Alexandra, as we all know, is not able to walk very far, and would not be fit enough for a long hike. Alexis is a non-starter, he looks as if he's had it. No one really knows what's wrong with him, but our man says he looks more like a death's head every day.

"Well, boss, that's the set-up. Four girls, who could maybe escape, out of the seven of them. It doesn't seem worth you coming all this way, does it, seeing that they can't succeed to the throne anyway."

The boss shook his head, frowning.

"We've spent weeks getting here, using resources on this job which could have gone on fighting the enemy. Do you mean to say that after all our time and effort, with Reynolds and me tearing round the whole of Russia, you could only come up with half the family, and the least important ones at that?"

Theodor sucked his teeth and nodded. Major Tierney looked at William, and back at Theodor.

"And these perishing girls were supposed to be here for us to collect today. What are Reynolds and I supposed to do? Make ourselves and the aircraft invisible, and eat fresh air in the forests for weeks on end, while you and your chaps fiddle about trying to get them out of the house and all the way here? For goodness' sake, man, you've been working on this thing for months. What's the matter with you all? Don't you want any of the emperor's family to escape?"

Theodor mumbled, "Everything has taken longer than we thought it would, boss." He sighed, leaned back, and spat heavily over his shoulder.

The boss went silent, staring at the ground. William knew him well enough to keep quiet, and spent the time trying to think of something. Theodor whistled through his teeth until William glared at him. Then the boss spoke again.

"Well, you and your contacts are going to have to get any escapers here without direct help from us. We can pass for Russians, but we don't know the town and I'd prefer we stayed with the aircraft. How long do you need? Two days? A week? A month? And are you certain that four people, the four girls that is, is the absolute maximum that we will have to transport?"

"Oh yes, the other three certainly either can't or won't escape. But I'd like a week. My contacts in the house are both good men and I can vouch for them completely. As it's not necessary, they haven't told me exactly how they plan to get the girls out. We've arranged that I will pick the girls up outside the fences in my lorry and drive them to a safe house, where we'll keep them in the cellar for a bit. There are bound to be searches as soon as the escapers are missed at the roll-call which they have every morning, and that means all hell will break loose, there'll be a security clampdown, and getting in and out of the area will be impossible for at least a few days."

"Why can't you drive them straight here after they get out of the house and into your lorry?"

"With the curfew being strict already, any lorry out and about after midnight will be searched, and if I was caught with the girls, everybody would be executed right away: them, the rest of the family, their servants, and me and all my family and relatives too."

"Right."

"If the reds haven't found the girls in the town after a week I hope they'll either give up or start looking elsewhere. Then I'll be able to bring the girls to my farmhouse in the lorry, and they can stay there till you come back for them."

"Right. Well, we can't stay here now. We'll go back to our camp and sit tight. Let's move the marker trees now so that they're at right angles. Today week we'll come back at dawn. If you've got the girls here with you and it's safe to land, lay the trees parallel. If not, leave them at right angles, and we'll not land but go away and try again in another week. We'll do up to three more weekly tries after that, weather and civil war permitting, and then we'll assume that things have gone wrong for you and we'll leave. If you have got the girls, but couldn't get them here to be picked up by us, it'll be up to you to get them to the railway and on their way to Vladivostok."

Theodor nodded. "Right, boss, I understand all that."

"Have you got enough money?"

"Not a lot."

"Here, take this. It's all I can spare and if we do pick the girls up I'll need most of it back for our own journey."

"Right you are, boss."

"Very well, let's check that all is clear, and get the aircraft out, and we'll be off. Hope to see you in a week, Theodor, and best of luck with getting those poor girls away from that perishing prison house."

Escape Night – Olga

Tatiana argued with Anastasia.

"Even if an escape chance did come I'd rather stay with Mamma and Pappa," her little sister said. "I don't believe the bolsheviks will dare to harm them. They're bound to send us all away to live in the Crimea eventually."

And she wouldn't budge, despite all Tatiana's clever arguments about what the four girls might do if an hypothetical attempt were made. The elder two were glad they had not told her that there was an actual plan in its final stages and just about to come to fruition. Marie wanted to join the escape, and Tatiana stopped her from telling Anastasia by saying Vladimir forbade it.

Vladimir told Olga to warn the other two escapers not to worry when they heard the guards having a party and shouting about fire during the evening of the 30th June, but to remain calm and try to pacify the rest of the family while being careful not to give away anything about the escape plan.

At midnight on 30th June 1918, the other two made Marie go first because she was the youngest.

She got down the back stairs and along the narrow, dingy corridor to the back door, which to her infinite relief, turned out to be open as Olga had promised her the men were going to arrange. She peered out, and then slipped out of the house, and there, she saw, was the familiar figure of Mikhail by the gap in the inner fence. He ushered her through both fences and across to Theodor, and she climbed into the lorry to burrow down among dusty sacks, trying not to sneeze.

Tatiana went next, carrying nothing, wearing her old repaired clothes and shoes, creeping quietly but quickly along the family's corridor. Never had it seemed to take her so long to get past all those doors. She headed towards the bathroom, so as to look innocent. She passed by the door and looked round. All was quiet up here even though she could hear shouting and banging noises coming up from the front hall downstairs, and there were some whiffs of smoke. "Good," she thought, "our men have got the other guards well and truly distracted." At the top of the staircase she took a last look round; all seemed safe, and she flew down the stairs.

Hall a minute later Olga peered carefully towards Anastasia, noted with relief that her little sister seemed to be asleep, and crept out of the girls' bedroom. She was trembling and depressed, and knew that she would be caught. For one moment she almost turned back, but her mind was so ground down that she could not face the agony of even one more instant of indecision, so she followed the plan as set even though she did not want to, not even comprehending that in so doing she might endanger the other two girls who she knew were already on their way out.

Heading past the bathroom door, she heard no movement, but four feet from the top of the stairs, there were heavy footsteps. She jumped and turned, to see three guards rushing at her from the end room. She just had time to think, "Hell and buggeration, Vladimir said that room was going to be checked," when two of them seized her, while the other one blew his whistle and yelled for reinforcements.

Shocked, she stood still, a pitiable figure, in her worn clothes, thin from strain and poor rations. The guards loomed over her. She heard shouts from the big staircase, and trembled when she saw Rudolf, a senior guard, stomping along with five more ruffians at his heels. She had always dreaded him most of all the guards, finding him both vicious and creepy, and knew that in return he loathed the sight and sound of her. She hoped Tatiana and Marie would get clear away, and felt an instant of grim humour as she realised that her being caught would distract the guards for a few minutes and give the other two girls a better chance. For a second she prayed that Tatiana would not endanger everything and everybody by waiting for her. Rudolf glowered as he came down the corridor towards her, preceded by a cloud of alcohol fumes.

Nicholas shouted from his locked room, "What's going on out there?"

Rudolf ignored him and stopped a foot from Olga.

"What's all this then, going for a walk in the middle of the night? Don't you like your wonderful living conditions in this excellent house of the people?"

Olga was too frightened to speak. Anyway, she wanted him to shoot her so that she couldn't give away the others and he might do so more quickly if she said nothing.

The guard clutching her left arm too hard replied, "We caught this useless enemy of the people off the beaten track, comrade, heading towards the far end of this corridor, near the back stairs. Doesn't look as if she was planning to leave us though, does it? She's got no coat nor luggage."

Rudolf glared down at Olga, and bellowed, "Roll call. Now. Get those useless Romanov leeches and their entourage lined up. Come on, move it. And you, MISS Olga Nicolaeivna Romanov, are going to tell us what has been going on around here, and it'll be too bad for you if there's been any escape attempts or like subversive nonsense."

With Rudolf leading and the eight other guards round her, Olga was led back up the corridor towards the family's rooms. The others were already all awake, and the guards began to usher them into the corridor. Then a guard rushed out of the girls' room, hustling Anastasia in front of him and looking frightened.

"Comrade sergeant! Two of the girls aren't in their room."

"What do you mean, what the hell, you little bitch," he turned to Olga. "Where are those bloody sisters of yours?"

Olga trembled but stayed quiet. He marched up until his face was an inch from hers. "Well, where are they?"

Olga wanted to say, "Got out of your miserable clutches," but hoped to keep silent for a few minutes yet to give the other two a better chance. She had no illusions about resisting questioning, and she was afraid of betraying Vladimir and Mikhail too.

She mumbled, "I don't know," but her innocent expression did not fool Rudolf. He stared hard at her face, so she looked down at the floor, afraid that he might read the truth in her eyes.

He decided that questioning her could wait, and turned to counting the others. Nicholas had been helping Alexandra into her wheelchair, and pushed her out of their room into the corridor. Before he went back to help Alexis out, Olga saw him looking puzzled. "You're wondering where the other girls are? Well, you'll soon find out," she thought viciously. The four servants were mustered, and joined the erstwhile imperial family for the roll call.

The prisoners were lined up with their backs to the wall, facing the corridor windows. To keep them on edge, Rudolf took out his list slowly, pausing several times to look up and down the line. "You slimy reptile bastard, playing with our nerves like that," thought Olga.

"Citizen Nicholas Romanov," roared Rudolf, making everybody jump. Nicholas was used to it. "Present", came his quiet voice.

Rudolf strolled over, looked his former emperor up and down, spat in his face, and went back to his gang. It was obvious that some Romanovs were missing, and Olga was hardly daring to breathe. "Please God make him shoot us all now so that I can't betray Tatiana," she thought.

Then a memory came to her, of standing on the threshold of their room, with Marie beside her, when she had arrived at this house. She had looked into the room, and known with total certainty that this was the last room she would ever sleep in. "Well," she thought, calm now that she knew her death was certain, "I just hope they make it quick and soon." The thought of dying did not bother her, except that she deeply regretted the end of her hopes of helping her country of Russia. But for herself, she looked forward to a better, happier life, sometime in the future, she thought, feeling glad that Brother Grigory had taught them about reincarnation in the old days. Brother Grigory! What a host of memories the thought of him brought up, and especially that strange question he had asked her, so many centuries ago. Yes, their old, dear friend had been right. "Do you think you will have many more years in which to carry out your duties?" he had said, and she had stared at him, puzzled. He must have been seeing her future here now, in captivity, and with no more hope.

"Next, the right royal tart, yes, I mean you, your graciousness, Madam Alexandra Romanov no less." Olga held her breath. Rudolf knew Mamma found roll calls one of the worst things about their captivity, and he was daring her to defy him. Olga hoped that he would get furious and shoot them all there and then, but there was no such luck. Mamma managed to say, "Present."

"Present, comrade," corrected Rudolf.

Alexandra gasped. Too defeated to speak, Nicholas took her hand and squeezed it. "There you go again, always preferring life to honour," Olga thought at him, sourly if a little unjustly.

"Present, comrade," snapped Alexandra, trembling with rage.

"Serves you jolly well right; if you'd gone out among the people twenty years ago and shown them that you cared, you wouldn't be here like this now," Olga thought, with an excusable lack of filial piety.

Rudolf had humiliated Alexandra and that was all that he had wanted.

"Miss Olga Romanov," he proclaimed.

"Present, comrade."

"Yes, Miss Olga Romanov Comrade, I can see that you, your mighty royalness, are present, but where, might I humbly ask, are Miss Tatiana Romanov and Miss Marie Romanov? Are you going to tell us your humble servants where your two useless lady sisters have gone? What were you doing down by them stairs? Wouldn't have been trying to leave this house of the people, now, would you?"

"I don't know," mumbled Olga, frowning at Rudolf's jacket.

"She doesn't know," announced Rudolf to everybody, shaking his head slowly. "She doesn't know."

Olga was glad they were all in a line, but wished she could see her parents' faces. Pappa would be wondering where the other two girls had disappeared off to, and Mamma will probably throw a fit, she thought, not caring, in fact, hoping that Mamma would throw a fit because it might distract the guards from hunting so hard for Tatiana and Marie.

Rudolf checked Anastasia, Alexis, and the four staff, then stared at Olga for five minutes. She didn't care. She felt he knew everything, and she was going to die soon now anyway, so nothing mattered any more.

"Okay, comrades, let's go," he decided. "Comrade Valentin and Comrade Alexander, you stay and guard these useless scroungers. Shoot anyone who moves." He and the others marched off.

The two guards rocked on their heels, lit up a cigarette between them, and stared at the prisoners. Olga swallowed. Accustomed as she was by now to abuse and silly rules, this really was a departure. That sod Rudolf did think up ways to annoy them, she thought, almost admiring his creative ingenuity. Again she felt sympathy for these men. She knew that they were badly fed because she had the same food. And their wives, Russian women just like her, what did they find as food nowadays, as clothes, supplies and things for their families? She hoped all those women out there managed somehow, but doubted it.

She thought back to her nursing days and how the war had changed their lives. The stories she and Tatiana had heard from the soldiers had been terrible, oh dear, the thought of Tatiana cut through her. Where was darling, wonderful little Tattykins now? Was she even alive? She stopped her racing thoughts, and sent out a firm prayer, "Please God, let me know!" and waited, forcing her mind, in desperation, to shut up for a minute. Her efforts were rewarded, by a tiny beam of light energy coming into the top of her head, and the thought came, "Yes," just one word, but enough. Then, she saw inwardly, with remarkably clarity, a vision of Count Worthton, standing a few feet from her, his kind, intelligent look focussed on her. "It's him, how wonderful," she thought, "He knew I'm desperate about Tatiana, and God let him come and tell me! Thank you, Monsieur le Comte! And thank you, oh Almighty God, for sending your wise and saintly emissary to tell me that my dear little sister is alive and well!" She prayed quickly and politely, even while she felt sad at the way that she and Tatiana had been parted.

Never again would she smile as her sister walked into the room, full of interesting talk. Never would they sit together, trying out new fashions and shoes and everything that all young ladies everywhere liked to enjoy. They had been more like twins, doing everything together, giving each other support in everything from lessons to fashion to suitable young men.

Not that they had seen much of young men, because Mamma had kept them so isolated. Realising she was heading for another session of criticising her parents, Olga forced her mind back to her family here in the corridor, and the guards leaning against the wall enjoying their dominance. She did not dare to stare at them, because this would have been called insolence. How well she knew their funny little ways. If she ever got out of this, she would write her life story, but it would never get published because no publisher would believe a third of all the weird stuff she would put in.

Voices shouted downstairs, and twice, groups of guards came up and rechecked all the rooms. Olga did not see Vladimir, and hoped that he and Mikhail had got right away. The prisoners stood and stood, until Olga lost count of time. She was desperate to sit down. She was still run down after their illness last year. Things had got worse from then on, and she had just had the strain of the escape. All right, curse the bastards, let them punish her, she hoped that they would not punish everybody else, and she sat down on the floor. Nicholas and Anastasia blinked down at her, concerned, but Alexandra was miles away and did not seem to notice and Alexis was too ill to notice anything.

Nothing happened. The guards carried on staring at the family, and Olga could not understand why they did not shout, get aggressive, or burst into those offensive revolutionary songs. Olga shut her eyes, saying to herself that she was just going to rest a little and wouldn't go to sleep, but on seeing her relax, the guards came to life.

"Oy!" The one on the left banged his gun on the floor. Olga groaned inwardly, and stood up.

"That's better, your royal lowness, MISS Romanov," said the other. "We can't have you destroyers of the people's revolution relaxing and enjoying yourselves, now, can we?"

By now Olga felt terrible. Shock at losing touch with Tatiana, and despair at their hopeless position, overcame her, and she fell flat in a faint.

She revived to find Anastasia rubbing her temples, her father kneeling by her, and Mamma clucking reproachfully. The floor was hard, and she felt as cold as death. Something was covering her, but not making much difference. She closed her eyes and opened them, to see in front of her Anastasia's knees covered in worn skirt. Olga remembered everything and groaned to herself, hoping she had not caused a huge amount of trouble for the rest of the prisoners. She moved her head, but the corridor lurched and she felt even more sick so she tried lying still. How weak and cold she was. She remembered Guard Rudolf had gone away, leaving them standing there like dopes. When would he come back, and how could she possibly fool him? Where could she find a knife and kill herself, she wondered hazily, desperate not to give away the escapers or the loyal guards.

"Come on, Ollikins darling love, are you there?" asked Anastasia. "You gave us all a fright and Pappa and Mamma are worried."

"Sod Pappa and Mamma," thought Olga, feeling too weak to curse out loud. She could do without that pair of idiots getting worked up. Anger at her father's failure gave her energy, so she propped herself up on one elbow and looked round slowly, not moving her head. The guards were lounging against the wall. The servants, bless them, were still lined up, looking exhausted, beside the family. The guards must have been threatening them. She felt sorry for them. They were so loyal, those four, and had come with their erstwhile employers to a miserable fate ending in death. Tears prickled behind her eyes and she sighed at the uselessness of their devotion. Anastasia lifted her up, and gave her a nice big hug.

Then what she had been dreading began to happen. Shouts and the sounds of heavy feet came from the main staircase, and she recognised Rudolf's voice. Now what was going to happen? He would have long since noted how the girls looked after each other loyally. She was sure he had worked out that the girls had been plotting together, and he must have realised by now that the two missing at roll call had got away from the house. If only she did not feel so weak, she would run off down the corridor, hoping they would shoot her. But her muscles were leaden, she was fighting dizziness, and she could hardly move. The heavy bootsteps of the guards made the wood floors shake, and echo hollowly. "Like a tomb," she thought, and trembled inside.

"Here are the contemptible and degenerate enemies of the people," Rudolf was saying. He sounded less arrogant than usual and Olga wondered why. He came up and loomed over her.

"Get up, you insolent slut," he roared, and made as if to kick her.

Nicholas acted at last, and stood himself between Rudolf and Olga.

"These women are my daughters and I will not stand for you committing acts of physical violence against them." He managed to sound a bit braver than of late, thought Olga. Pity he wasn't brave ten years ago. She waited to see what would happen.

"Here, stand to order, you lot," said a new voice. Along came a short, dark-haired man, with sharp features. Olga wondered where Rudolf had dug him up from at this hour of the night, no, good heavens, surely it must be nearly morning by now. Looking worried, Rudolf hustled the Romanovs back into line, Olga clinging to Anastasia and Nicholas, Alexandra staring blankly at nothing, and Alexis just managing to stay on his feet.

Rudolf mustered his heavies behind him, and stood beside the new man.

"Comrade Zukovsky. These are the worthless prisoners and enemies of the people. This is Nicholas the blood-drinker, arch-enemy of all that is good and worthwhile about our noble revolution. This is his common slut, the German traitor and spy, Alexandra, formerly mistress of the evil so-called monk, Rasputin. This, and this, are two of their despicable common wench daughters. This little fool is Alexis, former heir to the former throne of our great country. These others are four of the unfortunate and deluded palace hangers-on of Citizen Romanov. Foolishly they refuse to join us and come into the brotherhood of new, free, revolutionary man, preferring to remain loyal to their outdated notions of service to their emperor and his self-indulgent and greedy family."

Rudolf ran out of steam and stopped. "He looks pleased with himself, doesn't he," thought Olga. "He must have enjoyed getting the chance to insult us all in one go."

Zukovsky looked up and down the line of prisoners, counting.

"Comrade, you say two females have got away?"

"Yes, Comrade Zukovsky. Nicholas the parasite leech is famed for his four daughters. Here are two of them, but the others cannot be found. We have searched with great diligence and are certain that they are not now in this house of the people, nor in the garden. However, this one, former grand duchess Olga, was found in this corridor by comrade guards, there at the end near the back staircase. It is possible that the young women plotted an escape, keeping the others in ignorance."

"Show me your list of names, please, comrade. Thank you. Now, Nicholas, Alexandra, yes, the middle two females are missing. You say this one, Olga, may have been plotting. Why do you think this, comrade?"

"We comrade guards have been observing the prisoners, and have noticed division arising among the Romanovs. The older girls accused Nicholas the slayer of the innocent workers of allowing the spy Alexandra to rule the land and plunge it into war. One guard overheard Olga complain to Citizen Nicholas that he stopped the girls trying to escape from Tsarskoe Selo, their initial house of captivity. Thoughts of escape were still clearly on their minds even now, despite the disciplined imprisonment that they are now properly experiencing in this house of the people, and I regret that we have not kept them safely confined awaiting the people's decision on their future."

"What do you propose, comrade?"

"I suggest that we execute the remainder as a lesson to other enemies of the revolution. Or question the traitor Olga about this evening's events. I am sure that my men would find it most entertaining to question this treacherous lady Olga. Or alternatively I suggest that we execute Nicholas tomorrow, Alexandra the next day, and so on, to assist traitor Olga's memory."

"Comrade, your zeal for harsh measures may yet trip you up. It is essential that we all remember Comrade Lenin's orders, that the Romanovs are to be kept unharmed for use as counters for bargaining with imperialist enemy countries. I must proceed to Moscow immediately and report this loss of two of them. Reinforce the guard using local comrades, who I am sure will be very happy to assist. I will arrange their wages when I return. I will be back within a week, and in the meantime you are all to remember this: the Romanovs are to be kept unharmed. That is an order direct from Comrade Lenin and myself." He handed the list back to Rudolf, who started to heave a sigh of relief, then turned it into a deep breath.

"Your orders are understood, Comrade Zukovsky. I and my comrade guards will be attentive in our duty towards the revolution."

Zukovsky walked off down the corridor and as he disappeared down the stairs Rudolf looked as arrogant as usual again. He and his crew leaned on the wall and stared at the line of prisoners, who by this time were wilting with exhaustion but too frightened to move. "Who does he think he's frightening," thought Olga, but she was half asleep and almost forgave Rudolf because she could hardly remember anything any more except that she only wanted to lie down and rest.

After another half hour, Rudolf had had enough of annoying the Romanovs and decided to give himself some time off.

"We good citizens have to get up for work tomorrow, unlike you layabouts. We've got better things to do than stare at your ugly faces. Back to your rooms, now, and if anyone's heard talking, it'll be the worse for you."

He banged a gun on the floor. The prisoners jumped, and hurried to their rooms. Anastasia looked at Olga and was going to ask questions, but Olga waved a fist and she shut up. They were in enough trouble, and Olga wanted to think. She was kept awake by the guards talking loudly and stomping about. But eventually she nodded off, exhausted, and dreamed of rushing after Tatiana along a narrow basement corridor, with bolshevik soldiers wearing huge heavy boots and enormous patched greatcoats rushing after them.

The atmosphere among the prisoners next morning was frostier than Olga had ever known. She did not care. Knowing that she was going to die soon, she looked at Nicholas with contempt when he demanded, "What have you girls been up to, plotting escapes behind my back?"

At last she got brave enough to tell him what she had really thought of him for over a decade.

"I hate you, Nicholas Alexandrovich Romanov, eternally and irrevocably. If it had not been for you, this my country of Holy Mother Russia would be a harmonious light to all the nations. But instead she is a sodden rag full of death and ruin.

"I now curse you in the name of spirit, of honour, of loyalty, of love and of patriotism. I curse your body, your mind, your soul and your spirit. I want to see you rot in misery for many lives. You are abject and despicable beyond all words. All this is your fault and you are a mass murderer, a mass rapist, and a butcherer of millions.

"You and you alone are responsible for the destruction of not only what good Russia was manifesting but also the tremendous good which she could have manifested.

"You and your wife together have conspired and have brought down what could have been the world's greatest nation.

"You talk about God's Will. You never had the wit to see that God does not come down and run the world for us. He expects us to run it for him. But in your monstrous stupidity and arrogance you sat back, and allowed everybody round you to tell you what to do, and presumed that they were God speaking to you.

"Can you not see that God gave you a brain to use for yourself? You say, 'God save Russia', but can you not, did you not ever, realise that it was your job to save Russia?"

Olga paused for breath. Nicholas, Alexandra, Anastasia and Alexis were looking stunned. She leered back at them, feeling drunk with the pleasure of showing her hatred for Nicholas at last. She finished,

"It's a pity someone didn't assassinate you back in the eighteen-nineties."

Sounds of clapping came from the corridor, and in walked Rudolf and his two pet heavies. He bowed to Olga.

"Well said, Miss Citizen Olga Romanov. That was a splendid speech and I couldn't have put it better myself."

Olga stared at him. She was tempted to say, "Look, comrade, it's time I joined your revolution." She looked at him with new eyes, noticing the lines on his face, and the scars which, she knew, were a relic of his time in a metal smelting works. And she felt a compassion and understanding for him, with a mixture of shame at her family's part in the sufferings of his people – her people – and a longing for things to get better for his millions of comrades. But she couldn't bring herself to take the step. She had heard tales about how the bolsheviks treated women, even women who were pro-revolutionary; gang rape was all in the day's work, and she was less badly off the way she was, an imprisoned Romanov. She let the moment pass, but regretted it later because her only interest in the universe was Russia's welfare and maybe, maybe, the revolutionaries could do a better job than her lot, the Romanovs, had done. Well, she hoped so.

Escape Night – Tatiana

Tatiana always remembered hiding in the alcove, peering up the narrow staircase, and seeing Olga get caught, surrounded by that uncouth gang of gigantic, stinking guards. Too sensible to throw away her life in vain heroics, she left her sister, and rushed away fast before she could be tempted to go back and make a foolish, hopeless attempt. She was too keyed up to feel emotions about it at the time, but a corner of her mind knew she would feel it terribly later.

She hared along the downstairs passage to the back door and peeked out, but couldn't see any guards or disturbances, so Marie must have got away, thanks be to God. Opposite her was a gap in the fence. She ran to it, peered through, and saw Mikhail, looking worried. Waiting for Olga had made her a minute late.

"Where is the other lady?"

"Caught by guards in the house."

Mikhail grimaced. "The first lady got through. Here, madam, take this," and he handed her his tiny week's wage, a little money in a screwed-up piece of newspaper. Touched, Tatiana stowed it in her clothing. Mikhail saw her through the outer fence and she ran to the lorry. Mikhail would close the gaps in the fences, rub out any footprints, lock the back door, and hide the illegally copied back door key. Theodor helped her into the back of the lorry, then ran round to his cab and drove off. Tatiana hung on inside as the lorry bumped and lurched, and as she burrowed among the sacks, she saw Marie's head appear from hiding.

"Tatiana, oh thank God, but where's Olga?"

"They caught her. She was just getting near the top of the staircase when I heard footsteps and caught a glimpse of guards who must have been in the end room, grabbing her. There were three of them and there was no point in me going back up to tackle them all, and getting caught too. That stupid bloody fool clown Vladimir said he was going to check that the room was empty, so I don't know how he slipped up because they must have been in there for quite a time. Probably sneaked up there for a quiet drink."

"Oh my God."

"Too drunk to notice us two, but revived just a bit too much by the time Olga was going past the door."

"Yes."

Neither girl could speak. Theodor drove like a maniac and they hung on, each deep in grim thoughts. Four minutes later the lorry stopped, the driver's door banged, and Theodor appeared.

"Ladies, come out."

The girls clambered down, and found themselves in a small courtyard, in front of a two storey urban house. Tatiana realised they must be still in Ekaterinburg, and bit her lip, regretting that they were not at least out of the town. But she realised her rescuers were doing their best so she waited, alert and ready to cooperate with their instructions. A man and a woman, neither of whom she knew, stood within the doorway of the house, and Theodor took the girls over to them, saying,

"Dmitri and Naina will hide you while the bolsheviks search the town for you ladies. This will take some days, so you must stay very quiet while you are here and follow their instructions to the letter or you and many of us will all be executed by those accursed revolutionaries. For everybody's safety, at the moment I will tell you only that you will be contacted again later." He hastened back to his lorry and drove away. Dmitri closed the courtyard gate behind the lorry, and returned to follow the womenfolk into the house.

Naina led Tatiana and Marie in to the big, shabby kitchen, to where the cellar slab was open on the floor and a ladder led into the depths. The girls stared in concern, but climbed down the ladder. Naina came too, to brief them on arrangements.

"I'll bring you hot food when I can. Getting extra rations would lead to suspicion when I go shopping, but we've got a bit in reserve. We've done what we could to arrange beds and other facilities, and candles, and books for you to pass the time."

She looked at them again.

"I thought that four ladies were coming."

"The young one didn't want to risk it, and the eldest one was caught."

Naina looked distressed. "Oh, I am so sorry, ladies." She paused out of respect.

"We do appreciate very much that you and your husband are taking a tremendous risk in helping us," began Tatiana.

Naina shook her head.

"Madam, to us you are and always will be our emperor's daughters. But my husband insists that at present we use just your names, as titles would be dangerous. I do hope you don't mind."

"Oh, no, on the contrary, we agree that that's very sensible. I'm Tatiana and this is Marie."

"Very good, and I am your Aunt Naina and my husband is your Uncle Dmitri. In case of a really pressing emergency, bang on the hatch and shout, but try not to, because of the searches. Meantime, God bless you and we are honoured to have you in our house."

Naina went upstairs leaving the ladder in place, and closed the hatch on the girls. They looked at each other.

"Let's see what they've left us," said Tatiana, "and then I'll tell you what happened after you got out."

The two girls settled into a routine. They chatted quietly, said daily prayers, and read books; luckily Tatiana had still got a watch so they tried to keep regular hours. Tatiana insisted they do exercises, to keep fit in case of needing to do the long walk which Vladimir had warned might be necessary at some time during the escape venture. Dmitri and Naina let them up late each evening to walk in the courtyard, and they inhaled the fresh air with relief. The second day, the house was searched by a troop of bolsheviks, tough local men determined to hunt down their detested longtime enemies. The girls sat in the dark, frozen with tension and praying silently as heavy bootsteps, shouts and crashes echoed down into the cellar for over half an hour. But God preserved them and the revolutionaries eventually left, swearing loudly and smashing a window to vent their frustration at still not finding the Romanov girls.

Early on the sixth morning, Naina summoned them up out of the cellar, where they found that Theodor was back and was waiting for them in the kitchen.

"The bolsheviks have finished searching the town now, ladies," explained Naina, "so it is safe for you to move on."

The girls hugged and thanked Dmitri and Naina, and collected their meagre belongings. Back in Theodor's lorry, they felt him going round corners, and then settle into a long straight drive. Two hours later the lorry stopped, and the girls got out of the back to find they were beside a farmhouse, in a part of the country which they did not know. Theodor led them into the house.

"My wife has taken our three little girls south to her mother to get away from the civil war, and so for the short time that you ladies will be here you can use their bedroom. You can walk about in the house, but don't go outside in the daytime at all, but if it is safe I'll let you out for a short breather at night. I've got food, been collecting some extra, and can give you one or two of my wife's garments. Again I won't tell you any details in advance, for your own safety, but I will just say that another vehicle is due to come and take you further soon provided that the fighting lines don't get too near."

"Very well, Theodor, we will follow your instructions and I must say we are very grateful to you and your friends for all your trouble and risk," said Tatiana.

"Your room is upstairs, turn right, and it's at the far end. Now if you'll excuse me I must get back to work." Theodor went out.

Escape Flight

"I can't help thinking of those poor girls," William Reynolds frowned over his hot beef drink. He and Major Tierney were at their camp fifty miles east of Theodor's farm. "I suppose we keep trying as arranged, and then give up and leave; we can't hang about for ever."

"Well, my boss said we'd got to be out of Russia by the end of September," said Major Tierney, "and no reasons were given, although he must have them."

"Yes, so you've said," agreed William. He wondered again who the boss's boss really was; could it be King George the Fifth himself? He had never dared ask, not least because he did not need to know, but it was not unknown for the Monarch to trust specialised or controversial jobs to men whom he quietly chose himself without going through normal armed forces channels. The King was a former full serving member of the Royal Navy, and as well as being at heart a tough sailor himself, he knew a useful network of very handy individuals whom he could trust to tackle all sorts of jobs both official and unofficial. Thus pondered William as he thought about what he and Major Tierney were doing; after all, they were trying to save the King's own close cousins, in the teeth of well known opposition from factors in the British government who cared nothing for the unfortunate Romanov family and preferred to see them all perish, than try to save them publicly and thereby, so they claimed, risk upsetting various sections of the British public. William admired again the tough-mindedness of the King, knowing that if the story came out, things would indeed be stirred up by anti-monarchists in Great Britain. "Loud-mouthed traitors," muttered William, who believed that no system of government was perfect but that constitutional monarchy was by far preferable to many other systems which humanity had thought up.

The week dragged by. The men took it in turns to sleep, keep watch, and go for short walks. Every day they checked the aircraft visually, although they dared not start the engine in case the noise was overheard and brought curious people along. The weather was mild and damp, which meant that the temperature was comfortable for them but the insects were ferocious. The small camouflaged tent was adequate, and Theodor had left plenty of fuel and food so they were saved from the temptation to venture near to villages or towns. The men soon finished the three Russian novels they found in the cache, and resigned themselves to long periods of sitting peacefully contemplating the local flora and fauna. A nearby stream provided vital water and they also tried to catch fish in it to liven up their food supply, but they caught nothing except one or two tiddlers which were hardly worth frying.

On the seventh morning, William, whose watch it was, woke Major Tierney while it was still dark.

"Well, this is where the fun starts again," muttered the boss, sipping his hot drink. "Here's hoping we can pick up those wretched girls this morning. If we don't get them out soon it's curtains for them all."

The men had been listening to the distant guns for the past few days, but due to staying away from human habitations they had not seen any newspapers, and did not know whereabouts the main lines of fighting had got to.

They took off, and soon got near the rendezvous, Theodor's field.

As they flew, they noticed running figures and puffs of smoke. To save time, the boss had gone up to only five hundred feet, well below the layer of strato-cumulus, but high enough to be safe from rifle shots.

Getting near, the boss descended, and they arrived over the field at two hundred feet. The two trees were laid parallel.

William could not immediately see anybody, and assumed that Theodor and the girls were hiding, if they were in the field at all. Two fields away were tiny figures, their faces staring up. "Those must be the line of bolshevik troops," thought William, "my heavens, they are getting near; we're going to have to do this by the skin of our teeth and get out pronto." He assumed that if the fighting men below had been the friendly, pro-monarchist forces, the so-called "White Russians", Theodor would not have needed to summon the aircraft to pick up the girls. The boss turned and pointed at the figures. William did a "thumbs down" gesture to indicate bad luck, and the boss nodded.

Satisfied with his reconnaissance, Major Tierney turned the aircraft away from the field again, and William realised he was going to settle into his final approach to land. Theodor had promised to make sure the field was smooth, and William felt confident that the aircraft wheels would not hit a stray stone. The aircraft shot over the last hedge, the boss keeping the aircraft as low as he dared. Gently they touched ground, and the boss headed for the trees while William kept up a good lookout. The trees got nearer. The engine roared. Fifty yards from the trees the boss throttled back and the aircraft slowed. William stood up, and left his helmet and goggles on the seat. Now, where were Theodor and those girls? It was going to be a tight squeeze, and even if they could fit two girls in at a time they would have to make a minimum of two trips from this field back to their remote and hidden camp. How they would manage a second trip if there were bolsheviks stamping around all over Theodor's farm he could not imagine, but they would have to worry about that if it cropped up.

The aircraft turned to the right and drew up beside the two fallen trees. At last Theodor popped up, and William waved to him. The boss was keeping the engine running. He turned and nodded. William climbed down from the aircraft, and rushed over to Theodor, avoiding stray branches. With

Theodor were two pale, poorly dressed women, who looked quite old, and William stared at them, appalled, realising that it was suffering which had aged them so severely. Were these the elegant young ladies whom he had imagined? And why were there only two of them?

"Where the hell are the other two women?" he snapped in Russian.

Theodor shrugged and looked up at the sky.

"The poor ladies did not get away; one refused to come, and the other was caught within their house of captivity."

William uttered a strong oath under his breath, and then looked at the girls.

"There are soldiers two fields away and they are probably bolsheviks so you've got to get the dickens out of here now, immediately. Can you run to the aircraft?"

The thinner woman nodded. "Yes."

"Right then, come on. Theodor, help me get them to the edge of the trees, and then keep yourself hidden."

William offered his hand and the thin woman took it. He hustled her towards the aircraft, Theodor helping the other woman along close behind them. Something hit a branch near William's head and he jumped. He heard a shot from in front of them and realised Major Tierney was firing at the bolsheviks to slow them down, as even a minute or two was going to make all the difference.

"For heaven's sake, come on, that lot are shooting at us."

They rushed the last few yards. Theodor disobeyed William and stayed with the girls. They got to the plane. The girl with Theodor was stronger than the thin one and climbed in. A bullet hit the top wing and everyone jumped. The boss opened the throttle a little.

William and Theodor had to push the thin girl up the two indented steps. William had noticed her gasping for breath. The last he saw of her, she was falling in on top of the other woman. The boss opened the throttle. William waved thumbs up to tell him that it was safe to move, and dived with

Theodor into the trees. The aircraft turned, and zigzagged a few yards, bumping a bit on the grass. When it got up speed, the boss opened the throttle fully, and went for the take-off. William took a deep breath as the aircraft flew away towards the north-east.

The bolshevik soldiers close by assumed that everybody had got away in the aircraft. Like soldiers throughout history, they were happy to have an excuse to stop rushing across fields, and they called a tea break. William and Theodor hurried back to the farmhouse unmolested. Later some of the soldiers arrived at the farm demanding to search it, but William was by then safe in the cellar, and Theodor's long-standing act at being a devoted communist held up under their questioning, so the intruders' search was half-hearted at best and they left without finding anything. Theodor waited for another hour as a precaution in case the soldiers tried to trick him by coming back, then he let William out and brought out his best liquor to celebrate.

"So thank God at least two royal ladies have got away. Let us pour a little slug, William my friend, and drink a toast. To powerful bullets and straight shooting!"

"Straight shooting." They downed their "slugs".

"Now let us pray that they eventually get to Vladivostok all right through all the mayhem which those accursed bolsheviks have loosed upon our country. I hope that your great King George will be able to send another ship and that it'll have better luck than the one he tried to send to Murmansk earlier for the whole family. Then, they will be on their way safely."

"Yes. But I'm still hopping mad that we didn't get the others out. Is there any chance for them, do you think, Theodor?"

"No. None at all, my friend. They are finished and I just hope the reds kill them quickly instead of slowly, them and those wretched staff who would insist on being loyal."

"Have you had any more contact with our men at the house?"

"Two days ago I met Mikhail in the town. He's keeping a low profile at the moment. He said that after the two girls got out, the prisoners were even more closely watched and their food was cut down again. The whole guard troop were sacked, and a new crowd of jumped-up civilian thugs from the local mines were brought in. This is very bad for the prisoners, and also means that we no longer have him or Vladimir in place near them. No, I regret to say," he downed another large 'slug', "Our dear respected emperor and his family are shortly to become no more than a memory. The final curtain has now fallen on the Romanov dynasty of Russia."

"Yes, I'm afraid so. Things have got as bad as they could be. It sounds as though there's no point in my staying in this area any longer."

"No. If you're hoping to help the Romanovs any more, forget it. I know you'll feel you're letting the side down, but you have to face facts, old son. There is no hope for the ones still held in Ekaterinburg."

William nodded sadly, frowning, and stayed silent for a minute. Then he went on,

"How will the bolsheviks react when they find our camp, as they are bound to do, sooner or later if they haven't already?"

"I wouldn't worry about that. It was all standard army gear which I'd nicked from various places months ago, and there was nothing there that they could associate with the escape of the two girls. They'll probably assume it was stolen, and being used by deserters. But to be on the safe side, I wouldn't go back near there if I were you."

"Right."

"When do you want to leave? I reckon the sooner the better."

"I might as well go now and use the daylight. Can you let me have any money?"

"I've got most of what your boss lent me. I didn't get the chance to give it back to him, not surprisingly, so here's most of it but I'd like to hang on to just a bit."

"Fine, Theodor, thanks. Well, cheers, old son, and may you always have a well-loaded gun and a full larder. If you're ever in London, do look me up via the central army office and we'll knock back a slug or three together in a nice little pub I know near Piccadilly."

"You're going now then?"

"Yes. As you say, I think the sooner the better since there's no more I can do here."

"Can I give you a lift to anywhere in my lorry?"

"No, thanks, that's good of you but it's too risky, you've got a wife and family to think about, and it's possible that group of thugs will be keeping a close watch on this area for a bit. Don't worry, Theodor, I'll look after myself."

"May the road be straight before your feet."

They shook hands and clumped each other on the shoulder. From the door, Theodor watched William stride across the yard and go through the gate. William turned for one last wave, then he looked at the Sun, and strode away eastwards.

Rudge Plans a Trip

Rudge was wondering if he really was getting old. Two of those damned Romanov women had got out, under the very nose of his own pet special agent, that fool supervisor, Guard Rudolf, and were heading for freedom. Rudge would have had the rest of the Romanovs executed there and then as revenge for the humiliation, but he had heard that Comrade Lenin still insisted on keeping them alive as political bargaining tools, and Rudge had to admit to himself that there was a good deal of sense in this. His mistake had been in not frightening Rudolf into doing a better job, so he would have to consider organising an accident for Rudolf shortly. Yes, maybe he was getting old, so he had better be more careful from now on.

But, he checked his self-criticism. He had done well really. Within the past couple of years he had managed to infiltrate Comrade Lenin back into Russia against all odds, and prodded one of his main tools, that stupid empress, to make Nicholas do all the wrong things, or right things, he should say, right things, to make the revolution start. Blood was flowing freely all over Russia, his masters were pleased with him, and the future looked bright. Might there be promotion coming his way? Men were supposed to serve the dreaded Twelve Men solely out of devotion, but Rudge knew that one of them was getting old. He meant to be in the right place at the right time and seize the moment, and then he really would be on his way to ruling the whole world the way he wanted it to be run. Anyway, he was now the leading power in Russia, one of the half dozen biggest countries. Yes, life was good, and he had done it all by himself, with no bowing and scraping to some God or other. Oh, no. Rudge stood on his own two feet and made sure he earned the rewards he wanted, so that things came to him in the way and at the time which he himself had planned.

At the March 1917 revolution he had disbanded the empress's magical group because he did not need it any more. To hide his tracks he got most of the members killed by some of the goodly number of men in and around St. Petersburg who were desperate for any kind of work to earn a few honest or dishonest coins. His crowning achievement, which he still felt hugely proud of, was fixing the murder of that interfering "monk", Grigory Efimovich Rasputin-Novykh. Rasputin had been a worthy enemy, and Rudge had to admit that while he was alive he had caused a great deal of trouble, fighting to keep Emperor Nicholas away from disaster, and even trying to make Nicholas keep Russia out of the world war which he, Rudge, had plotted and schemed for. Rudge would have liked to get his longtime arch enemy, Count Christophe Worthton, Rasputin's magical controller, lined up in his sights and safely out of the way too, but the confounded man had a knack of vanishing at any sign or even thought of trouble. Neither Rudge nor his agents in Russia had seen a sign of him for months, but Rudge could not believe that Worthton had left the country permanently, it was in too much chaos, and limiting the chaos which Rudge spent his life trying to create was one of Worthton's specialities, curse the fellow.

Rudge sat back in his favourite padded chair, and rested his feet on another one. He sank into a reverie, and sat staring at the bookcases lining the walls in the salon of his St. Petersburg apartment. The revolution was jogging along all right, with plenty of mayhem everywhere, and he was beginning to feel he could safely take a bit of time off to go and accomplish what he had been planning to do for a long time, namely, kill that fool Nicholas with his own hands. He'd go to Ekaterinburg and see about taking a pot shot at Nicholas and those other idiot Romanovs, sooner rather than later. All right, Comrade Lenin had commanded that they be kept alive, but Rudge still had an uneasy feeling that some more rebellious of their worker guards might organise a convenient accident for them all. And he wanted the joy of executing Nicholas himself, not hearing that someone else had done it. After all, he had been waiting enough thousands of years for this moment of satisfying revenge. And if he was quick about it, he could do the job and get clean away long before Comrade Lenin heard anything about it.

Lost

At two o'clock in the morning on the 17th July 1918, the members of the Romanov family still in captivity were feeling mystified as they sat in the dim, echoing front hallway of the Ipatiev house in Ekaterinburg. They were worried about their four loyal servants, taken away earlier, and sat in silence, so cowed by now that they did not bother trying to converse as they knew that this would bring instant punishment, usually loud foul language with threats of physical assault, down on them immediately. A short volley of shots rang out from the basement, then shouts and footsteps. The Romanovs jumped in dread, and looked at each other, terrified. Three guards appeared from the back of the hall and strode across to them. Past caring about himself by now, but worried for his former servants, Nicholas asked,

"What was that noise? Nothing to do with my valued staff colleagues, I hope?"

The leading guard grinned, and one of the others answered,

"Mind your own business, Mister Romanov, you'll find out soon enough, just what that noise was all about."

These men of the new guard troop, brought in after the escape of the two girls, were even more uncouth than the previous crowd. Nicholas shook his head and did not bother to say any more. His family looked at him with sympathy.

Someone banged on the door. The dominant guard frowned, and he and the other two strode over and opened it. The guard conversed for over five minutes in a low voice, and the Romanovs could not catch what he was saying, but he sounded nervous and servile. Olga looked across discreetly, but could not catch sight of whoever was outside.

She saw the guard nod, and then he blew a whistle, and six more men appeared from the back of the hall as the three came over to the family from the door.

"Right, you load of imperial excess baggage, traitorous imperialist troops are getting near, so you are being moved away from this house of the people."

The Romanovs did not bother asking where to. They picked up the small bags they had been allowed, and Nicholas started to push Alexandra's wheelchair across towards the door.

"Oy, Mister Romanov. That chair is staying behind."

"But my wife needs it all the time."

"That's too bad. There's no room for it in the lorry. The right royal tart is going by stretcher and so is your precious clown tsarevich. Right, comrades, bring those stretchers and get these redundant spongers off the people up on to them. Make sure you are really nice and gentle with our precious ex-emperor's darling family."

The guards heaved and shoved the two sick people, while Nicholas tried to make them be more careful, but eventually a guard pushed him full in the chest so that he crashed over backwards, and just missed banging his head hard on the stone floor. Olga gasped and rushed over to him, feeling slightly guilty over the way she had been railing at him lately, and he gratefully accepted her help to get up slowly, testing for broken bones and nodding at her to indicate that he was all right. The guards plonked Alexandra and Alexis on the worn old stretchers of thick, ancient cloth, and carted them out and into the back of the lorry; for Alexandra it was one of the worst moments of the whole period of imprisonment, with the humiliation worse than the discomfort.

Still holding her father's hand, and reaching supportively to Anastasia as they followed her mother and brother out of the hall door, Olga glanced at the new man as she passed him. He was tall and gaunt, with dark hair which looked somehow too young for the rest of him. She plucked up the courage to look into his eyes, and she shuddered. His eyes were completely colourless, and reminded her of a beast of prey. He caught her gaze, and as he looked deep into her soul she felt that he was some frightful primaeval leviathan on a dreadful mission of destruction. She knew suddenly that he was one of the chief architects of Russia's miseries, a great monster of evil, clever, calculating, and young in mind while ancient in years and knowledge. Once again her rage at being deprived of the Russian throne surged through her, and then, she remembered the wisdom of Count Worthton, and how his tuition had helped her to learn that there were some things which she simply could never change, no matter how much she wanted to, and no matter how much she worked and prayed. Still, she was going to die soon now anyway, so all that was left for her to do for her beloved Russia at this stage was to offer her death as a sacrifice, and to hope that God would consider her worthy enough for her blood to be used to build the country up in some way against the cataclysm through which it was now passing.

She and Nicholas jumped up into the back of the lorry and tried to help Alexandra and Alexis. Anastasia was crying with exhaustion. As the family tried to arrange themselves more comfortably, a canvas cover was flung across the back and the small amount of light shining across from the hall of the house was cut off. The lorry started, and they were all flung about as it bumped and swayed. Olga was sure that the driver was being deliberately rough in order to hurt them, and they all clung on grimly to each other or to anything they could reach. After ten minutes of frightening chaos, the lorry stopped far more abruptly than it needed to and the canvas cover was moved back. The tall, gaunt man, who seemed by now to have taken over, stood well back, watching, and the three guards from the house who were acting as his assistants, plus half a dozen other uncouth heavies, swarmed towards the family.

"Out," snapped one of the new men, and the Romanovs who were fit enough helped the guards to remove the invalids from the lorry. Olga sighed as she remembered again for a second the prophecy of Brother Grigory, "You will have many ends, each one more diminishing than the last," and then she forgot it again as she looked round cautiously. They were at a railway station, standing right next to a train which looked ready to depart, with steam up and a couple of railwaymen looking out from the engine compartment expectantly. Olga wondered if those men knew who her family were, and speculated to herself about what was going on. Who was this tall gaunt man with the frightening eyes? He had appeared out of nowhere but seemed to have taken control over their guards, and why was he removing them from the Ipatiev house in the middle of the night, on to a train bound for an unknown destination? Some order from "Comrade" Lenin, she supposed, and mentally shrugged.

She jumped to help as the guards moved them to the train, and clambered in with her family and six guards. Thank goodness, she noted, one of the guards was carrying a lamp, so they would not all be sitting in pitch darkness for maybe hours. The large wood door in the carriage wall was banged shut, and sealed from the outside, and Olga, who had always suffered from being closed in, swallowed nervously. There was shouting from outside, and loud hissing from the engine, and then with a lot of clanking, the train began to move. The Romanovs looked at each other in the dim light, not daring to speak but hoping to gain courage from each others' familiar faces. Olga blessed herself and Nicholas followed suit. Anastasia seemed to be in complete shock, almost beyond crying, Alexandra was looking a mixture of furious and exhausted, and Alexis was pale and more gaunt than Olga had ever seen him, glaring at the floor and biting his lip with anxiety.

After four hours of uncomfortable boredom, the train stopped, the door was opened, and the prisoners who were able, were allowed to climb down for fresh air. Olga took some much-needed deep breaths, and then peered around hopefully, but they were somewhere in one of Russia's interminable forests and she could not begin to guess where they were. After ten minutes they were ordered back in again, and for some reason the guards, who had previously been eating and drinking merrily in front of them without offering them anything, now presented them with stale water and equally ancient bread, which they consumed gratefully. The train rumbled on, and Olga began to lose count of time.

Around mid-morning the train stopped again, and the Romanovs blinked gratefully in the daylight as the fit ones helped the invalids down from the carriage in a deserted railway station in what seemed to Olga to be a fair-sized town, although she could not work out exactly where. The guards who had travelled with them hurried them into a lorry which had been standing waiting, and the Romanovs resigned themselves to yet another session of dangerous, uncomfortable jolting. But the journey only lasted a few minutes, to their relief, and when the lorry stopped and they were hustled down they found themselves in the enclosed courtyard of a small old brick town house. Ten ruffians lounged round the door, and they and the guards got together to talk while the Romanovs waited, the two invalids still on the stretchers and all of them untidy, hungry and tired. For ten minutes the arguing went on, but then a decision seemed to have been taken because with some final shouting the guards who had come on the train with the family went back to the lorry and drove off, and the new lot ordered the Romanovs into the hall of the house.

The tall gaunt man appeared again and Olga wondered how he had got there apparently before them. Had he come on the train? She watched him guardedly, not daring to look at his eyes again. He dominated the guard troop, who all seemed wary of him, and brushed past a couple of the men contemptuously as he strode over to speak to the family as they waited, flagging, in the dim hall.

"You unwanted scum have come to your last house. Welcome to Perm, and this is where you now stay. We, the great Russian people, desire only vengeance against Nicholas and all of you and we will execute our vengeance in the way which we have decided. You will stay upstairs unless ordered, and food will be brought to you if or when we so please. And in answer to your question, Citizen Nicholas Romanov, you may be very pleased to know that your servants were indeed executed at the house of the people in Ekaterinburg."

He walked away and his cronies pushed them upstairs. Nicholas and Olga tried to carry Alexandra up the stairs, then Anastasia came to help, and they only just managed all right because even though Alexandra had got thin from the bad food, they had too and were weak and unable to carry much weight. Then they made a second trip to help Alexis. Upstairs, everything had been looted; there were no carpets, curtains, or even bedding, but just beds with bare mattresses, four beds in one room and two in the neighbouring room. Olga remembered Brother Grigory's words again, "You will have several ends," and thought, how right he had turned out to be. She felt terribly sorry for little Anastasia, just a young girl and now doomed to die. At least she, Olga, had seen a bit of adulthood and even though that had been hard going, with the war, her detested nursing spell, and then the revolution, somehow she felt that her young sister's coming death was much more tragic than her own. It was happening with Anastasia at such a young age but old enough to have more idea of what might have been than a little girl would have had. Olga was beyond exhaustion, but as she intuitively felt now that she was going to die within hours rather than days, she decided to spend her last bit of life helping her family, and with that decision, a last surge of energy came to her. She rallied round and helped her father settle Anastasia,

Alexandra and Alexis as well as they could, and then she lay down and slept.

About sunset, she woke, starving but feeling better for the rest. She hoped that an evening meal might appear, but it did not even though the family were tormented by food smells coming upstairs from the guards' kitchen on the ground floor. There were three guards on duty by the top of the staircase, but they sat around and didn't harass the Romanovs, and they let them visit each others' rooms, the two girls in one, and Nicholas, Alexandra and Alexis in the other. Olga was nervous. She felt the guards were waiting for something. The family all gathered in the larger room and did some quiet praying, and the guards still did not harass them. After a couple of hours, Olga and Nicholas plucked up courage and asked them about food. The men stared at them, and one said, "What do you want food for?"

"But we're starving," said Olga.

"So what? Due to your inhumane policies and cruelty to the workers and uncaring bad management and useless greed, Russian comrades and their children are starving. Now it is your turn, and we men of the people hope that you will enjoy starving. You'll be fed when we see fit and if you harass us again you'll be chained in the cellar."

Nicholas and Olga gave up and went back to their rooms. Olga did not talk to Anastasia much, there seemed to be no point. She recited all the psalms she could remember, and dozed off again.

Transition

When they were woken again it was dark. Olga could not work out what time it was, but she felt that she had been sleeping for a couple of hours and it must be around ten or eleven.

"Right, you lot, come downstairs."

"For crying out loud, can't you let people have a decent rest?" muttered Olga, pulling her shoes on furiously. The half dozen guards produced a wheelchair from somewhere for Alexandra, and the three stronger Romanovs carried her downstairs, unsurprised that the guards stood around watching and did not offer to assist. Nicholas and Olga went back and helped Alexis down the stairs to the hall, and they were all hustled towards the back of the house, down a few steps, and into a semi-basement rear passage. After a few yards they arrived in a small empty room with old yellow wallpaper, a hard earth floor, and two small windows of which one was barred.

The tall gaunt man came in, and the six guards with him filled the small room. They stood behind their leader as he spoke to Nicholas.

"King Nikolay, I have waited for this moment for thirteen thousand years."

Olga wondered what he was talking about, and for a moment forgot about her own impending death through sheer curiosity as she stared at his face hoping for some kind of explanation. He carried on addressing her father as though no one else was there in the room with the two of them.

"Do you remember Atlantis, King Nikolay? Do you? I do. And I have waited and plotted for this moment for thirteen thousand years. Oh, yes. In those days I swore vengeance against you for defeating me, Verion Rudge, in battle when I was the greater man in the lands. And I have been pursuing you ever since, planning and creating the opportunity for this my moment of ultimate triumph. Thirteen thousand years. You cannot conceive of this length of time, can you. But I can. Long since I became a great master of the magickal arts and sciences, and I have been alive in this body which you see now for over five hundred years. I have pursued your soul for many lives. I have manipulated and checked your soul. I have held your soul when it suited me, and then let it go again when it suited me. I have made you take the actions which I wished you to take. We have been linked, you and I, for many of your short pathetic lives. And even as every action which I take always succeeds, my plans for vengeance against you, King Nikolay, have now succeeded most perfectly. You humiliated me in life, and now I will humiliate you in death. I will ensure that your failure as king and emperor will be known around this world forever, and that your name will become a by-word for weakness and lack of moral fibre. Prepare to meet your non-existent God."

He stood tall, enjoying his dominance, allowing the Romanovs time to feel fear. Then he raised the small pistol he was holding and pointed it at Nicholas.

Olga knew she was going to die in a minute, and her emotions stopped. She stared at the floor, wondering whether her blood would run over it or sink in, and remembered Brother Grigory again, and the times when he had told her and Tatiana that one's blood being poured out over the ground was a good magickal practice, creating protection for the country.

More men were pushing into the room, and one grabbed her, a short thin man with angular feature, dark hair, and big hands. She heard shots and saw her father fall over backwards. She struggled uselessly, but this man held a pistol, and there was such glee in his face. He fired at her from a yard away and she felt her nose and cheeks break up, but no pain, only awful shock. Suddenly she couldn't focus properly any more and she felt herself losing control over her muscles. As she fell backwards away from her attacker her right foot caught something warm, still and soft. It must be one of her family. Terror and grief raged through her. Where was everybody? What was going on? Then she fainted, and lay across the body she had stumbled over. Her consciousness floated away from her body, and she forgot everything. She and the others lost touch with each other.

If used in the right ritualistic way, the blood of an innocent young person can have very good magical effects. Olga's sacrifice was an example. Thanks to the specialised magical teaching given to her by Brother Grigory Efimovich, her sacrifice was made voluntarily and with conscious mind knowledge, which added tremendously to its power. This power was further enhanced by her sacrifice being made with the knowledge of her higher mind, at a vital time, and in a drastic way, killed by the enemies of her country.

Due to Olga's knowledge of the Devic Kingdom, her blood sacrifice worked throughout the Devic realm as well as the realm of human energies.

In the last few moments, she had been too fraught mentally to think of the Great National Deva of Russia, but because she had worked with him previously, this Deva Master had a permanent mental link with her. Unless he was especially busy he could detect when she was under particularly dire stress, even though this did not necessarily lead him to take any action about it.

However, he detected that she was about to die, and so he left his other work of continual energy manipulation, in order to take and use the energy which she wished used for the welfare of Russia.

A few minutes before her execution, the Deva in all his invisible power and splendour arrived in the sky near Perm to await her death and the consequent spilling of her blood, which he knew would provide him with a large amount of fresh, high quality spiritual energy with which to bless Russia and enhance its protection. To the normal human eye he remained invisible as ever, but to an advanced human clairvoyant eye he would have appeared as a vast four-sided pyramid, deep grey in colour, with fire in the middle, and with sides three hundred feet long meeting at a point which shone like a crystal lit by fire from within.

Devas are not subject to human emotion, so he did not feel grief. His feelings at that moment were more like a human being's deep concentration on the job in hand. As Olga was shot he saw her blood flow over the ground, spilled by the enemies of this country of which he was a guardian, and he saw spiritual energy rise from her shed blood like steam to form a cloud. Olga's blood sacrifice worked throughout the Devic realm as well as the realm of human energies. It caused a fusion of human and Devic energies which exploded from the physical plane through the higher and lower planes of existence. Not only human beings can perform rituals, but Devas can too, and so the Great Deva took these energies, and manipulated them for his country's welfare, scattering them among holy places like tiny refreshing drops of silver rain, Olga's devotion helping him to form the blanket of protection which he held in place over the land.

This work done, he returned to his dwelling place in the spiritual heart of Russia. The place which he considered to be his main dwelling was located, in physical realm terms, to the west of the River Lena. This was his main centre of operations; here he dwelled invisible and all knowing, doing his best to help Russia with the small amounts of good energy which were all that the human beings living in the country provided him with, compared with the vast amounts of contaminated energy they threw at him by normal everyday human selfishness, wickedness and stupidity.

Even though Olga was expecting to die, when it happened it felt unexpected, and the unexpectedness felt merciless. She was anaesthetised by shock and horror, and waited around, hovering in the cellar, for quite a time. In front and to her right, near her, were all the bodies. She recognised her father and felt a pang. She had ended up hating him in life, and what she had craved for, for so long, had happened – he was dead. But she was dead too, and it was all pointless now. He and her mother, sister and brother lay in heaps. Vaguely she recognised her own body; she knew it by the old coat and shoes. She looked for the face, but there was nothing there. The jailer had shot her point blank right in the centre of her face. She felt shock when she saw it, but only distantly. The body had been hers, but it was no longer relevant now. Something seemed to have numbed her.

To her left was the crowd of assassins. There were so many of them. She felt resentful as she looked at them. Why had they needed to bring in so many? Oddly, she felt that it all would not have been so bad if there had been fewer executioners. But this huge crowd, why, there must be nearly a dozen, and there they all were, looking smug and vengeful. "I bet you don't know I'm watching you," she thought, but of course none of them reacted. The two dominant ones, nearest to her, the tall sinister one and his chief underling, were talking. She saw them approach the bodies, and move about, checking that everyone was dead, and felt they were discussing the disposal of them. She heard their voices, but the words were inaudible, as though coming from far away.

Suddenly she realised that a grey fog was closing in and wrapping itself round her. She hovered in the cloud, still stunned with shock. It was quiet, but she kept hearing the gunfire noise repeat itself over and over in her memory, and was shuddering with the horror of it all. There was a faint perfume, which made her feel sleepy, and it was cool and pleasant. She was drawn backwards, and her view of the cellar, with its tattered wallpaper, the curved beams on the ceiling, and the dim light, faded from her view, getting smaller and more distant as though seen through a reversed telescope. Then the fog closed in round her completely. It carried her silently backwards through the walls of the cellar, out of the house, into the garden, into silence and peace, and she was alone.

It was quiet and kind, this aloneness. If she thought, she could hear again the ranting of the murderers' voices, the terrible loudness of the few, oh so few, shots, that had carried her and the others away. But then she did not want to think any more. She let everything go and nothing was left, no memories, no sadness, and above all, no mental or physical pain.

Then, Olga had a vision. Among mystic islands far to the west, there was a chapel. She saw an alcove, and in it, holy symbols lit by coloured lights. Olga stared at it all, and was cheered by it. She was allowed to observe it for five minutes, and then she was drawn away. She closed her eyes, and her soul fell into a deep sleep.

The five Romanovs were buried in a small, remote quarry a few miles outside Perm, then covered with three feet of gravel. Rudge did not want monarchists finding the bodies and using them for power-generating magical rituals. He made sure that the world believed the Romanovs all died at Ekaterinburg, by murdering the men involved at Perm over the next few days. That was the end of King Nikolay. He had kept his vow of vengeance made so many millennia ago, and all in the line of duty too. He, Rudge, was a clever man. Satisfied, he began a leisurely journey back to St. Petersburg. He would make sure that the revolution was jogging along, killing enough people to satisfy his masters' desire for continual blood sacrifice, then put his feet up for a bit and start writing his memoirs.